AF486593

Giving him a shocked look, Anjali said, "Parth, what are you doing?"

"You tell me. What are you doing to me, Anjali?" he came back, tracing the shape of her lips with his thumb, an expression of intense concentration on his face.

Anjali shook her head, her hand closing over his wrist, trying to pull his hand away from her face. Only there was no strength in the fingers which encountered his skin. Her fingers traced the fine hairs on his wrist, while her thumb couldn't help but feel the pulse. It beat rhythmically against her finger, making her more aware of him than ever before.

It felt as if he was weaving a cocoon of magic around her. She wanted to simply shut her eyes and give herself up to his caresses.

"Parth!" her voice was choked.

"Anjali..." he whispered close to her ear, his hot breath stirring her nerve-ends. Her eyes shut in surrender when she felt his lips press against her temple. She felt him lift her from her seat and stand her on the floor, his arms going around her waist.

"Parth, this is not right," she protested, her heart not really in it.

"Just one kiss," he said, "I promise not to ask for more."

ABOUT THE AUTHOR

Sundari Venkatraman is an Indie Author who has 65 books to her credit. These books have consistently featured in the Top 100 Bestseller Lists on Amazon Kindle, in both romance as well as Asian Drama categories. Her latest hot romances have all been on #1 Bestseller slot in Amazon India for over a month.

AN AUTOGRAPH FOR ANJALI is a second chance romance with a thriller element, and is also a standalone novel. This kindle book remained in #1 Bestseller position on Amazon India for three months from its release.

Even as a child, Sundari absolutely loved the 'lived happily ever after' syndrome and she grew up on a steady diet of fairy tales, Phantom comics and Mandrake comics. It was always about good triumphing over evil and a happy ending after the protagonists surmounted all unexpected obstacles.

Once she entered her teens, Sundari switched her loyalties from fairy tales to Mills & Boon. While she loved reading both, she kept visualising what would have happened if there were similar situations happening in India; to local heroes and heroines. And of course, the joy of vanquishing the ubiquitous evil villains! Her imagination soared and she happily ensconced herself in a rosy romantic cocoon for many years.

Then came the writing—a true bolt from the blue! And Sundari Venkatraman has never looked back.

Books by Sundari Venkatraman

Standalone novels
The Malhotra Bride
Meghna
The Madras Affair
An Autograph for Anjali
Twin Torment
Finding Anya
Mr. Perfect
Man Friday
Her Prince Charming
Love in Agartha
Arjun's Penance
The Floundering Author
Ryan Finds a Bride
Tinder Loving Care
Shaan Gets Hitched
For Better or For Worse
Love… No Conditions Asked

Collection of shorts
Matches Made in Heaven
Tales of Sunshine

Marriages Made in India Series
#1 The Runaway Bridegroom
#2 Her Smitten Husband
#3 His Drunken Wife
#4 Her Secret Husband
#5 The Casanova's Wife
#6 Her Bohemian Husband

The Bansal Legacy Trilogy
#1 Simha International
#2 Rose Garden International
#3 Maharaja International

The Thakore Royals Trilogy
#1 The Marriage Predicament
#2 Tied in Knots
#3 The Wooing of the Shrew

The Groom Series Trilogy
#1 Groomnapped
#2 Gobsmacked
#3 Grounded

Written in the Stars Series
#1 Scorpio Superstar
#2 Leo's Desire
#3 Taurus Temptation
#4 Virgo's Krush
#5 Libra's Flame

Arora Iyers Trilogy
#1 Once Bitten Twice Lucky
#2 Heartthrob
#3 Call of the Heart

Dashavatar (Indian Mythology)
MATSYA: The First Avatar
KURMA: The Second Avatar
VARAHA: The Third Avatar
NARASIMHA: The Fourth Avatar
VAMANA: The Fifth Avatar
PARASHURAMA: The Sixth Avatar

**The Princess Series
(Historical Romance)**
#1 The Passionate Princess
#2 The Rebel Princess

The Writer's Toolkit (Non-fiction)
Publishing Your Book on Amazon KDP

Bollywood Bros Trilogy
#1 Sing For Me
#2 Dance With Me

Romantic Shorts
#1 *Chahti Hoon Tumhe*
#2 Beauty is but Skin Deep
#3 Madeinheaven.com
#4 An Arranged Match
#5 The Reluctant Bride
#6 *Shweta ka Swayamvar*
#7 Papa's Girl
#8 Red Rose Dating Agency
#9 Rahat Mili
#10 Reema's Matchmakers
#11 The Matchmaker's Dream

AN *Autograph* FOR ANJALI

A romance novel by

SUNDARI VENKATRAMAN

Love,
Sundari

FLAMING SUN

Notion Press Media Pvt Ltd
No. 50, Chettiyar Agaram Main Road,
Vanagaram, Chennai, Tamil Nadu – 600 095

First Published by Flaming Sun 2016
Printed & Distributed by Notion Press
Copyright © Sundari Venkatraman 2016 & 2023
All Rights Reserved.

ISBN 979-8-89133-776-3

Edited by: The Book Club Editorial Panel
Cover Illustration: Unaiza Merchant

AUTHOR'S NOTE

AN AUTOGRAPH FOR ANJALI is a romance, family drama, murder suspense all rolled together with some hot romantic sequences. At the end of it, it's a pure entertainer.

DEDICATION

I dedicate this book to the women from Venus!

ACKNOWLEDGEMENT

Thank you, *Advocate Ganesh Narayan* for your inputs on the workings of criminal law. Thank you for lending me *Principles and Practice of Criminal Law* by Shrikant Bhat for further research.

1

A siren pierced the morning as the police jeep arrived at the entrance to *Helios* in Hiranandani Gardens, Powai. The elevator whisked the Police Inspector and his deputies to the tenth floor. Stepping out, Inspector Phadke caught sight of a woman wailing as she sat on the steps leading up to the next floor. A couple of people were doing their best to calm her down. The door to the apartment on the right was open. It was Flat 1016A, what the police were looking for.

Phadke knocked on the door out of politeness before entering the large living room. A woman in her thirties was sitting on the sofa, still as a statue. There were two other people—a man and a woman. Phadke walked forward, catching the eye of the man.

"Thank you for coming, Inspector," said the man in a deep, cultured voice, "I'm Parth Bhardwaj, a friend of the family."

Phadke shook Parth's hand, saying, "I'm Inspector Phadke. I received a call..."

"That was from me, Mr Phadke. Please come," said Parth, leading the police officer to the left where the master bedroom was situated. Phadke looked at the woman sitting on the sofa, curiosity tickling him. She hadn't moved an eyelid since he had entered the flat. He followed Parth to enter a bedroom. The air-conditioner was on, while it looked as if someone was sleeping on the double bed. A closer inspection showed that there was no movement. Phadke walked to the bed as he saw the reason why he had been called in. Blood was liberally spread on the man's chest, while his eyes stared unseeingly at the ceiling. He wore pyjamas while the comforter lay beside him, unopened. It was obvious that he had been dead for at least a few hours, shot in the chest, close to his heart.

"That's Jayant Mathur," said Parth, giving a name to the dead man. The Inspector nodded silently in reverence to the dead and stepped out of the bedroom along with Parth.

"Is there somewhere we can talk?" asked Phadke, wondering how the woman sitting there was connected to the dead man. She had still not moved.

Parth led the inspector to the other end of the hall and sat him on a dining chair. "Who are the two women?" asked Phadke.

"The one sitting on the sofa is Anjali Mathur, Jayant's wife, the other woman is Sita, the cook," answered Parth, to the point.

"Who's the woman crying outside, on the staircase?" asked Phadke. She was the only one who appeared upset at the man's death.

"She's the daily help. Her name is Radha. Well, it was she who found that Mathur... well, she found Mathur in the morning," said Parth.

Phadke was curious as to why it was not the dead man's widow who had seen the corpse first, but he kept his thoughts to himself as he wrote down all the details in a small note book.

"Have you called for a doctor?" asked Phadke.

"The Mathurs' family physician is not in town. When I spoke to an assistant doctor, he told me that since Mathur was already dead, it was best if a police doctor checked him."

Phadke nodded, turning to one of the constables who had come with him. He instructed him in Marathi to call a police doctor who stayed close to the area. Then he spoke to Parth again, "I hope nothing has been moved in the bedroom?" People didn't really understand the meaning of tampering with evidence. They tended to trample on the murder scene—and it did look like murder to him—with the subtlety of a bull in a china shop.

Parth shook his head negatively, saying, "As I understand it, the maid Radha had knocked on the bedroom door a few times at eight o'clock. When there was no response, she had pushed the door open. Walking in, she saw Mathur, just as he is now, and ran out, screaming at the top of her lungs. The cook had rushed out—she lives in, by the way—of the kitchen, soon followed by Anjali, who came out of the *pooja* room which is next to the kitchen." Phadke turned to look at the respective rooms when Parth gestured in their directions as he explained the situation. Parth continued, "The two of them went into the bedroom to find Mathur dead. Anjali called me immediately.

I called you before I came over." There was no hesitation in his voice, as if he had prepared that little speech in advance. Then again, the man who must be in his late thirties appeared very confident.

"Where do you live, Mr Bhardwaj?" asked Phadke, continuing to make notes. He needed to get all the preliminary information in place before his senior from the crime department arrived. He hoped the doctor also had his report in place before that.

"I stay at *Olympus*, a few buildings away from here." Parth gave his full address and contact number to the inspector when asked. Phadke couldn't help noticing Parth's silver-grey eyes going to Anjali Mathur every few seconds, as if to check on her welfare. Well, it was not on his part to show curiosity about how people from high society lived. And it couldn't get any higher than this, he concluded, surreptitiously studying the furniture and artefacts in the room. The man must have been a millionaire, many times over. His mind ran at full speed in curiosity. He couldn't help but wonder if Jayant Mathur had been murdered for his money. His wife appeared beautiful, though she was as still as a statue.

"Do you think Mrs Mathur will be in a state to answer a few questions?" asked Phadke.

Parth nodded as the police officer got up to talk to Anjali. One thought was uppermost in Phadke's mind. *If Jayant Mathur had been dead since last night, where had Mrs Mathur been at the time of death? The half of the bed next to the corpse hadn't been slept in.*

2

Anjali sat in a stupor, quite uncaring of the happenings around her. She was in a state of shock. Just when everything was working to her advantage, just when she was on the threshold of finding happiness, this had to happen. Jayant had to die! Why? She was sure he hadn't committed suicide. Though, he did have a licensed gun kept in the drawer at the side of his bed. Who would have wanted him dead?

And how could someone enter the flat? Her mind boggled with unanswered questions. She caught Parth and the police officer walking towards her in her periphery. She waited. She knew they must have a lot of questions. And she had no plans to break down, not again. She hoped Arjun had caught a flight out of London. Her cell rang as if on cue. Seeing Arjun's photo on the screen, she picked up her phone immediately and placed it against her ear.

"Mom, my flight takes off in an hour. I'll be with you as soon as I can." Her son's voice broke at the other end as he mourned the early death of his father.

"You take care, Arjun. Have a safe flight," said Anjali, her eyes shining with unshed tears, unable to bear his pain.

"Is Parth there? I'd like to speak to him," said Arjun. Anjali handed her cell phone over to Parth and waited for him to finish talking. She saw Parth nodding his dark head several times as he spoke to her son in reassuring tones. "You don't worry Arjun. I'll remain with your mother right here, until you get home. You have a safe flight. I can pick you up if you give me your ETA." He paused for a few seconds to hear what the other man said before replying, "Okay then, no worries. I'll hold the fort at this end. You get yourself here," and disconnected the line.

Handing the phone to Anjali, he said, "Inspector Phadke needs to talk to you."

Anjali looked at the young police officer and gestured to the single sofa adjacent to hers. Sita served them all tea before Phadke spoke. "How do you think your husband Mr Jayant Mathur died, Mrs Mathur? Do you think it's possible that he committed suicide?" Anjali noticed that Inspector Phadke's tone was apologetic.

She shook her head as she replied, "No Inspector. Jayant didn't commit suicide. He's just not the type." He was—had been—anything but a coward.

Phadke continued to ask questions as he wrote. "Mrs Mathur, I can see that... er... the half of the bed beside Mr Mathur hasn't been slept in. You..." he hesitated, obviously wondering how to ask her about the couple's sleeping arrangements.

Anjali looked him straight in the eye, her own brown ones unblinking. "My room is on the other side," she said, pointing to the door which was diagonally opposite to the master bedroom. She didn't elaborate further. She didn't believe it was the police department's business if she slept with her husband or not.

Anjali so wished that her son could arrive sooner. Jayant's sisters and their families were on their way, having picked up his parents. She wasn't too keen to face the lot of them even if she could relate to their grievance. As for herself, Anjali felt a kind of apathy towards Jayant's death. Well, it was terribly sad that he had been murdered but—she couldn't stop the inadvertent sigh which rose within her—could Jayant have had an enemy from the business world?

Jayant's parents entered the apartment just then. His father Makarand who usually had an almost military bearing was almost doubled over in pain. His mother Chaya's face was wet with tears. A quiet woman, she was silently mourning her only son's death. The old couple walked forward and spontaneously hugged Anjali while she felt a bit of a fraud, having felt no closeness to Jayant since a long time.

She hugged his parents back, having no grudge against them. They may be old-fashioned and they may believe that men were the better species, but, despite all that, they had always treated her with affection.

Anjali looked over their shoulders to see that Smita and Nandita had followed with their husbands. She walked forward to hug her sisters-in-law one by one. Both were elder to Jayant and must be terribly shocked to know that their youngest sibling was no more.

Just as the lot of them were about to barge into Jayant's bedroom, Phadke's voice stopped them. "I am sorry Sir, Madam, you cannot all go in there together. Only one at a time, please. And you cannot touch Mr Mathur," he warned.

Anjali could see that the Inspector didn't mention that a policeman was stationed inside the bedroom, keeping an eye out. She wished the forensic team would arrive soon. She saw the shocked expression on everyone's face when they noticed Phadke for the first time. Smita's husband Rana asked, "Police? What's happening here?"

There was no way to break the news but to say it as it was. Anjali responded in a soft voice, "Jayant was killed." She couldn't get herself to use the word 'murdered'.

Makarand and Chaya were dazed. Rana demanded with a heavy frown on his face, "Killed? What do you mean killed?"

Anjali looked at him helplessly. She so wanted to save the old couple more trauma. She heard Inspector Phadke answer Rana, "Mr Jayant Mathur was shot in his chest at point blank range. We suspect it's murder."

A joint groan emanated from the six people who had walked in recently, their faces in different states of shock. Chaya gave a loud cry before falling down in a dead faint.

Just then the forensic team arrived. Everything happened in a blur from that point. Anjali watched on helplessly as an ambulance was summoned after the forensic team had completed their job. Jayant's parents and sisters cried bitterly while Anjali watched dry-eyed as they took away Jayant's corpse for post-mortem.

She wondered what she would have done if Parth hadn't been there, not just taking care of the formalities, but giving her the strength which she seemed to have lost along with the untimely and gruesome death of her estranged husband. While he went nowhere near her, it was still Parth's presence which kept her sane.

Arjun went into the washroom at the airport to splash cold water on his face. His eyes were red as they burned with unshed tears. He still couldn't believe his father was dead. Larger than life, loud and talkative, Jayant was—had been—a businessman through and through. Arjun had heard his father's success story so many times but never failed to be fascinated by it. Born from a lower middle-class family, Jayant had completed his BE and MBA with flying colours. Much to his father's shock, Jayant had started his own business instead of taking up the lucrative job offers which came his way. But he had proved to be a success right from the beginning.

Arjun looked into the mirror, wiping his face with a perfumed cold towel placed on a rack. While his forehead and sharp nose were replicas of his father's, the rest of his features were exactly like his mother Anjali's. A small smile tugged at Arjun's lips when he thought of her. She was lion-hearted. He wondered how she was taking Jayant's death. He couldn't make out much from her voice. She must be disturbed, of course. After all, they had been married for more than two decades.

He knew that his paternal grandparents had celebrated their golden wedding anniversary a few years back. But times were changing. Relationships didn't last that long. His mind went to Parth and again he couldn't help a small smile slipping on to his face. The man was a rock. Arjun was glad that his mother wasn't alone.

He heard his flight being called and walked out of the washroom, his haversack slung on his shoulder, his stride confident. No one looking at him would have guessed of his recent loss. Settling into the comfortable business class seat, Arjun shut his eyes.

4

arth refused to move from Anjali's flat despite the questioning looks from Jayant's relatives. He co-ordinated with the police and forensic people and he also arranged for Mathur's cremation two days later.

The press was another matter altogether. With great difficulty, Parth managed to keep them away from the tenth floor of the building. But that didn't stop them from stationing themselves at the entrance to the building and questioning every person going in and out. They were like wolves, baying for blood. They wanted to hang the murderer, pronto! They didn't care who got hurt while they aired their various opinions in print, TV and social media.

But Parth could be quite adamant when he set his mind to it. He hired a couple of bouncers to keep people away from the tenth floor. The only other neighbour on the floor was grateful that the fuss was at a minimum.

Parth could see that Rana was waiting to pick up an argument and he just refused to meet the man's eyes. It was obvious that Mathur's family felt that

Parth didn't belong there and it was they who should be in charge. But Parth couldn't give a damn. He was ready to face anything for Anjali's sake.

He couldn't help but admire her stoic behaviour. He was again amazed at how insensitive people could be. An author by profession, he was good at observing people. Mathur's old parents were totally shattered by their son's death, especially after hearing that he had been murdered. Chaya was a diabetic while Makarand had a heart condition. Parth had the devil's own time getting them to eat their meals regularly. He didn't want sick people on his hands now. Why the hell couldn't Mathur's sisters take care of their parents? It wasn't as if they were broken down with grief. He saw the four of them—Smita, her husband Rana; Nandita and her husband Deo—sitting around and gossiping. They were probably counting Anjali's worth.

Yes, Parth was extremely cynical that way.

He walked over to Anjali to verify the wording for the newspaper announcement to be given on Wednesday. He didn't notice Rana following him with Deo in tow.

Parth handed over the paper he had written on to Anjali. "I think it's best if this announcement appears on Wednesday. You..."

"On Wednesday? Why the hell? Today is Monday. It should come out in tomorrow's papers. Let me handle this," interrupted Rana rudely, trying to snatch the paper.

Parth turned his piercing silver gaze on the older man and said in clipped tones, "The autopsy will get done by the second half of tomorrow and we will receive Mathur's body back only by late evening. Do you want people to come over here before that?" Idiot, he refrained from adding.

Rana glared at Parth, refusing to back down. Parth turned back to Anjali and gave her the paper to read. She ran through the few lines and nodded to Parth, only to have Rana snatch the paper from her hand. Parth watched him with a frown as Rana read what he had written. Unable to find any fault with it, Rana made a big show of running the write-up through the other three.

After they had all finished reading it, Rana gave the paper back to Anjali as he told Parth, "Ensure that it appears in all the papers. We shouldn't..."

Parth nodded curtly before walking away, not wanting to pick up an argument in Anjali's presence. It wasn't fair to her if they bickered right now. Rana followed him and tapped Parth on his shoulder. "I am talking to you, Bhardwaj," he said sternly.

"I heard you, Rana. I just think we need to be a little more considerate towards Mathur's parents and the recently widowed Anjali," said Parth, the sarcasm evident in his voice. His anger had been simmering from the moment he got news of Mathur's death and he had been waiting to vent it. Who better than this foolish relative who talked big but helped none!

"Who the hell are you, Bhardwaj? How dare you insult me? What right do you have in Jayant's home? You are but a neighbour. I am the *damaad* of this house, do you know that? You can't treat me like this." Rana's voice rose with each sentence.

Parth's silver eyes gleamed like laser beams as he stared at Rana coldly. "I don't give a damn whatever you are. I'm in charge until Arjun gets here. You are welcome to take your rants to him." He turned away without waiting for the other man's reply, going about his tasks. There were too many formalities to be completed to hang around arguing with Jayant's relatives.

Parth met Anjali's eyes over the heads of the others, his gaze reassuring her that all was well. He watched her turn away to deal with her aged parents-in-law, his chest heaving in a soft sigh.

ana was furious, to put it mildly. When he married Smita, his brother-in-law Jayant had still been a student. The Mathur family had been from the middle-class. Despite that, Rana's parents had demanded fifty thousand rupees as dowry and got it too. It never struck Rana that his father-in-law had taken a loan to conduct the wedding. It was not as if he would have cared even if he had known about it. Being an only son and a graduate, Rana felt that it was his due.

He was a good husband to Smita and an affectionate father to their only daughter Ritu who studied in the USA these days. Which had been possible only due to Jayant's financial help. Rana couldn't have afforded it with his marketing salary. But then, Jayant was the kid's maternal uncle. It was his duty to help, wasn't it? Rana felt it was his right to take money from Jayant. And why not? Jayant had pots of it. That he worked hard to earn it didn't matter to Rana.

It was a few years after Rana-Smita's wedding that Jayant had set up his own business. Rana had insisted that Jayant was being extremely foolish. After doing an MBA, wouldn't it make better sense to take up a job with an MNC? He would surely have made more money from day one. He didn't speak to Jayant for a couple of years when the younger man refused to take his advice.

Soon, Jayant had proved his mettle as a businessman and Rana was ready to set right the broken relationship. It definitely paid to be friendly with a rich brother-in-law.

Rana didn't think very highly of Jayant's wife Anjali, though. He felt she was snooty. So, what big deal if she was beautiful! So were most women. Anjali kept to herself and that got under his skin.

Look at her now! Not a single tear for her husband of twenty years. Jayant's murder didn't seem to have disturbed her one bit. What kind of a woman behaved like this! And this Parth Bhardwaj—who the hell did he think he was? He went about the house as if he owned it. And Rana could see that the other man's concern for Anjali was a mite too much.

Rana wondered how to deal with the situation. Then light sparked. He would talk to Arjun. He was sure Jayant's son would understand. He would be the right person to chuck Bhardwaj out of the scene. With a smirk on his face, Rana went back and sat with his wife and other relatives, continuing to discuss the extent of Jayant's wealth. Yes, everything belonged to Jayant. He didn't think that Anjali had anything to do with it.

6

Smita was inconsolable, though she didn't show her emotions obviously. She was aware of her husband Rana's nature—how he was interested in only how much Jayant was worth. Not that it bothered her. That was how Rana was. But to Smita, Jayant was her little brother. She had been a few months over four years when her mother delivered Jayant. Unable to recall the birth of her younger sister Nandita, Smita had been fascinated by the newborn. She adored him from the moment their mother introduced the two of them. Brother and sister—in fact, all three Mathur siblings—had been very close. Jayant dying at the young age of forty-seven, that too in such a gruesome fashion—Smita couldn't digest it at all.

She felt choked. While she nodded and shook her head to the conversation going on around her, she registered none of it. The siblings had grown further and further away as each one got married. It was Smita's wedding which happened first. Despite a busy life in her own home, Smita always managed to spend quality time with her parents and siblings. It wasn't easy, but she still managed it. One good thing had been that they had all been living in Mumbai.

Why the hell would someone want to kill Jayant?

He had been an adorable child. Yes, he had been thoroughly spoilt by their parents and both the sisters too. But then, he was a rarity—a male child after two daughters. Smita and Nandita held no rancour when he was treated like God.

Anjali was nice and Smita got along well with her sister-in-law. Though she wasn't someone you could get close to. Smita looked at Anjali now. She was almost regal in bearing, sitting there like a reigning queen. Wasn't she upset at her husband's death? No remorse? She hadn't shed a single tear, at least, not in their presence. Had she been aware that something like this was going to happen? She didn't even seem shocked. She was unapproachable and hadn't said much except the basics. She had even answered their questions in monosyllables.

It was that neighbour of hers, Parth, who was doing all the talking. Smita eyed him curiously. Had he been Jayant's friend? Or—a thought slowly wormed its way into her mind—Anjali's? Oh my God! Had he been the cause of Jayant's death? Watching all those TV serials sure made Smita think dramatically.

She felt a powerful adrenaline rush, her sorrow forgotten for the moment. Though Smita had visited her brother regularly, she had never met Parth. She would have definitely remembered him. How could one forget those piercing silver eyes?

Radha entered the Mathur residence after seven days. She knew the funeral was over, though there were still a few relatives and friends around. She walked directly to the kitchen, without meeting anyone's eyes. She knew everyone's focus, especially the close family members, was on her. But of course, it was she who had first come upon Jayant's dead body. She shivered as she recalled the scene yet again for probably the hundredth time in the past week.

The police had been around to her home a couple of times, asking a lot of questions. But Radha had felt too ill to answer them coherently. She had been down with fever after the shock of discovering the murder and her non-stop wailing. It had been so horrible, coming upon her employer's corpse, that too with so much blood on his chest. His eyes had been looking up at the ceiling unseeingly. She had screamed so loudly, as she had never done before. She had been afraid that her heart would stop. The scene haunted her every waking moment. The doctor had given her sleeping pills as she didn't dare shut her eyes at night for fear of being haunted.

Sita turned from the gas stove to greet Radha. "How are you now? Your husband said you had been very ill all these days." Her eyes were kind, very understanding of the trauma the servant must have undergone.

Radha's eyes teared up. "What to do *Didi*? Why did this have to happen to me? Anjali *Bhabhi* and you live in this house. But unfortunately, it was me who had to find *saab* in that state," she sobbed, her body shaking. "The police keep coming to my house. My husband and children are also worried for me. Do you think they will put me in jail? I had nothing to do with it."

Arjun walked into the kitchen just then and heard Radha's words. Despite his grief, he felt sorry for her. "Radha *bai*, you don't worry about that. Of course, we all know that you didn't have anything to do with my father's death. The police just want to know what you saw when you entered the bedroom. I will call them here now. You give your statement and they will not bother you again. You take some more leave and get better."

Radha looked at her young master gratefully and sighed, nodding her head. As long as the police didn't knock on her door. And she could do with a few more days off.

"*Theek hai*, Arjun *baba. Aap kaise ho*? I'm really sorry that you returned home under such circumstances. It's so sad that a nice person like your father died in such a terrible way," she offered her condolences.

8

Arjun sighed, helping himself to some coffee from the large flask. He refused to shed the tears which were desperate to pour out of his eyes. He still found it difficult to believe that he would never be able to talk to his dad, not be able to dine with him, or share anything with him. His dad wouldn't be around for his graduation. Jayant would never be a granddad to Arjun's children when they are born. He walked away and stood on the tenth-floor balcony, staring down at the garden, unseeingly.

He didn't turn when he felt a comforting hand on his shoulder. He knew it was Parth. He just put his head back on the older man's shoulder, finding comfort. Without him, both Arjun and his mother would have gone to pieces. Whether it was the police, the media, relatives or friends, it was Parth who dealt with all of them. What Arjun liked best was Parth's don't-give-a-damn attitude when people tried to question his relationship with the Mathurs.

But all that didn't solve the mystery behind his father's murder. Why would someone want to kill him? It had been established that Jayant had been shot with a bullet at point blank range with his own pistol. Yes, the police were investigating further. But they could take forever.

Arjun turned to Parth. "Why don't we get a private detective on the case Parth? I don't think the police will find the murderer any time soon."

Parth looked at the younger man. "You may be right. Do you think there might be someone on your father's company's payroll? Or do you want me to find the right guy for this?"

Arjun shrugged; his eyes dull with pain. Shaking his head, he said, "I've no clue. We can ask Dad's assistant. Seema might know if there's someone."

"Hmm... not a bad idea."

"Let me call her," said Arjun, removing his cell from his jeans pocket. Seema's cell was out of reach. He called Jayant's office landline. It was answered immediately by the office attendant. "Ronak, this is Arjun. Can you please get Seema Dodhia on the phone?"

"Good morning, Mr Arjun. Seema madam is on leave. Do you want to talk to anyone else?"

"Do you know when she's coming back to work?"

"I don't know, Mr Arjun. Shall I ask and get back to you?"

Arjun realised that it didn't really matter when Seema returned from her leave. It wasn't his problem. "That's okay, Ronak. It's nothing urgent," he said, before disconnecting the line.

"I know a detective actually. I have used him to do some research for one of my novels a few years ago.

Give me half a day. I'll need to recall his name and unearth his contact details. I'm sure I have it in my laptop," said Parth.

"Thank you Parth," said Arjun, hugging him. "Mom and I couldn't have managed without you."

"Is this a vote of thanks? Are you sending me away?" joked Parth, smiling at Arjun. The boy could use some lightening up.

Arjun laughed softly. "Come on Parth! How will I survive? Or Mom for that matter," he grinned.

Neither of them noticed Rana standing outside in the hall, eavesdropping on their conversation.

9

It wasn't easy staying aloof with Jayant's parents and sisters living at home. It was worse with Rana and Deo also staying back. Especially Rana! The man was truly a pain, irritating everyone with his overbearing attitude. Why the hell didn't he go to work? Anjali was careful not to say much. Only she wasn't aware that she appeared all the snootier for it.

She felt sorry for Smita and Nandita. They were obviously upset about their younger brother's untimely death. It must have been such a shock. They seemed to be coping well though. But Anjali, being the honest soul that she was, couldn't pretend to a grief that she didn't feel for her husband's death. How could she? They had grown too far apart over the past many months. A few more months and Anjali would have shifted out of the Mathurs' family home. But then, she hadn't known that fate had had a cruel plan for her. Anjali's body shuddered with a deep sigh, unaware that Jayant's sisters and their husbands were discussing her cold attitude behind her back.

Anjali did her best to console her parents-in-law. She could so relate to their agony. Losing their only son must have been a terrible blow. And she hadn't been able to stop them from knowing that Jayant had been murdered. She had got their family doctor to keep a check on them every day. It wasn't easy making them have their meals, especially Chaya. She hadn't stopped crying, the tears silently pouring from her eyes which were permanently red. Her plump frame had shrunk badly over the week.

Then there was Arjun. He was heartbroken. Just because she had stopped loving Jayant, it didn't mean that her son's feelings had changed too. Anjali sighed! If she felt any grief at all, it was for her son's sake. Well, she hadn't wished her husband dead. But it didn't matter to her either way.

There! She had finally given words to her thoughts.

Yes, it was terrible that he had been murdered. Who would have wanted to kill him? And how had that person entered the house in the first place? It was obviously someone Jayant knew, concluded Anjali. The house was burglar proof and the alarm would have gone off the moment someone tried to enter their flat stealthily. The whole building would have heard it and so would have the police at the nearest station.

The murderer was definitely someone Jayant knew. Could it be an unhappy business associate? Jayant had got along with their friends and neighbours. She didn't see a problem there. Well, she had told the police everything she could think of.

Though they had organised a formal *baithak* on Sunday, friends and relatives kept pouring in to offer their condolences. Jayant's parents were in no state to meet so many people. It was left to Anjali and Arjun to deal with them. While Rana hovered around importantly, it was Parth who managed everything—ensuring that everyone was sent on their way as soon as possible after serving them tea or coffee, without seeming rude.

The newspaper hounds needed to be kept back from spouting too much gossip. Reporters and photographers from the media were stationed below the building. They were trying to chat up anyone and everyone who visited the Mathurs.

And people didn't seem to understand that it wasn't a fun shoot or interview. Some of them stood back to talk to the camera. Not that the media gleaned much from these footages.

Anjali refused to let any of it bother her. She knew that this too shall pass! Yes, she had become wiser as that was what life's hardships taught one.

Yes, the wife of an almost-billionaire had had to deal with her demons and it hadn't been easy. Just when she thought she was finally free of them, Jayant had been murdered. It looked like she had more to face before she found happiness.

But even she couldn't have guessed how much more.

10

Inspector Phadke looked at Rana Sahni, the brother-in-law of Jayant Mathur, the murder victim. Rana had gone to the police station along with his wife Smita. The lady looked pretty uncomfortable, wiping the sweat from her upper lip every few seconds. She hadn't opened her mouth since she entered the premises, allowing her husband to do all the talking.

Rana said, "I'm sure Anjali Mathur is having an affair with Parth Bhardwaj. Don't ask me for proof. That's for you to find out. I can only give you a hint. The two of them seem too close to be normal. And I don't really know what Bhardwaj does for a living. He has gone nowhere in the past few days and seems to have all the time in the world. For all we know, he's after Jayant's fortune and that's why he must have made Anjali stray towards him. It's one of them who has killed Jayant, I am sure." Rana's eyes darted this way and that as he spoke to Phadke, not quite meeting the latter's gaze.

Inspector Phadke sighed. Dealing with murder was difficult enough. That of a millionaire was trouble with a capital T. It was obvious that the relatives wanted an open-and-shut case, especially if they could establish the spouse to be the culprit. That way, they stood to gain more of the property. But they seemed to forget that Jayant Mathur had an adult son.

And Rana obviously had no clue about who Parth Bhardwaj was. That man was a famous author going by a pseudonym. He was ten times as rich as Jayant Mathur. Why the hell would he want the dead man's property? But about his relationship to Anjali Mathur — well, Phadke had had no clue. But it was only a couple of days back that her son Arjun and Parth had been to the police station. They seemed to get along well. Will Arjun share a rapport with the man if he was his mother's boyfriend? Phadke needed to think as there were too many things to assimilate.

He looked at Rana and said, "Thank you, Mr and Mrs Sahni. I will add your information to my portfolio and definitely check it out." He got up, indicating that the meeting was over and shook Rana's hand.

Rana looked as if he wanted to say something more, but Phadke turned to a constable and said, "Call that man who has been waiting since morning." He nodded to Rana in dismissal. Not having a choice, Rana walked out of the room, leading his wife.

There was no one waiting to meet Phadke who sat down to check the portfolio on the Jayant Mathur murder. He found a statement by Radha, the servant who had come upon Mathur's corpse.

Radha had said, "That Parth sir comes home often but only to meet Anjali madam. Yes, Jayant sir knows him also. It was Jayant sir who brought Parth sir home first. But after that, Parth sir became madam's friend. I have heard from Parth sir's servant that madam goes to his house everyday too." There was more gossip along those lines. The servant, who had been nervous about meeting the police, suddenly seemed to have a lot to say to them.

Phadke rubbed his chin, lifting the cup of tepid tea from his desk and drinking it. All these—Rana's and Radha's statements—were pure gossip. He couldn't conduct an enquiry based on that. But, as they say, there can be no smoke without fire.

11

Samrat took the call from Parth Bhardwaj on the second ring. He remembered the author and the research he had helped him with a year and a half ago. Smiling, he said, "*Bolo* Parth *saab*, what can I do for you?"

"Hello Samrat! Glad that you remember me. This time I want you to investigate a real case for me. You will need to come to Mumbai for that. A friend's husband has been murdered..."

Samrat heard all the details the other man had to tell him, making quick notes in the small book he always carried with him. He nodded and shook his head, listening carefully. "From the details you have given me, it looks like the victim knew the murderer," he said.

"Bulls-eye!" said Parth. "I hope you can come over immediately, Samrat. I know you have a busy schedule. But this case is slightly getting out of hand and I want you to find the murderer before the police bungle things up, helped along by the media."

"I understand Parth*ji*. I am between cases now and very much free to work on this one. Let me book myself on a train and call you."

"That's simply great Samrat. I'll book you on the earliest flight right now and mail you the ticket, you come directly over to my home. You can stay with me like the last time. Just in case, I'll also give you the Mathurs' address as I spend more of my waking hours here nowadays."

"Thank you so much, Parth*ji*. I'll pack immediately and await your email," responded Samrat before disconnecting.

He packed his bag methodically as his wife watched on. Was he glad that he had got to spend at least three days with his family! His detective agency was a one-man show, as he preferred to work by himself. If he needed help, he hired someone ready to freelance. He had just completed a case last week and was taking a breather. While his job gave him a lot of satisfaction with a lucrative income, it took him away a lot from his family. But Samrat, his wife and two kids had learned to live with that.

12

ana was excited, his eyes gleaming wickedly. It looked like the police had finally cottoned on to what he had known all along. Inspector Phadke had just walked in with a police woman in tow. He watched with glee at the drama unfolding in front of his eyes, while the rest of the family appeared shocked.

Inspector Phadke said, "Mr Parth Bhardwaj and Mrs Anjali Mathur, we have come to escort you to the police station. The DCP has some questions regarding Mr Jayant Mathur's murder."

Rana grinned. That Bhardwaj bastard had had it coming to him. And Anjali, well, she obviously deserved what she was getting.

Bhardwaj nodded to the policeman before turning to look at Anjali. Rana gritted his teeth. What was with these two? It served them right that the police were taking them in. He felt confident that the law would ultimately get to the bottom of the truth—that these two had perpetrated Jayant Mathur's murder.

Bhardwaj turned to give some instructions to Arjun; by what right, Rana couldn't fathom. He was unmoved when he saw the tearful Arjun hug his mother close. *Saali*, even now her eyes remained dry. Was she a woman or a vampire?

And Bhardwaj—the man seemed to hold both mother and son under his spell. It was high time someone brought some sense into the situation. Rana knew that Anjali would never listen to him. It was best to tackle the Mathur scion. Since Arjun would be the sole heir to Mathur's fortune, it would serve Rana best to befriend the boy.

The minute the police left with Bhardwaj and Anjali, Rana turned to the others, with a malicious smile on his face. "I knew it all along. Look at them both, so proud of themselves for what they have done. Never thought they would get caught, I'm sure. But the police are not fools, you know," he said to the room in general. He felt proud of the part he had played. It was he who had turned the police's head in the murderers' direction. What didn't strike him was that he wasn't going to impress Arjun by maligning his mother.

Rana turned to Arjun, who was looking anxious. He decided to add some fuel to the fire. "Arjun, I hope you don't mind my saying this," he paused, waiting for Arjun to give him his complete attention before continuing, "I don't trust that Bhardwaj at all. I'm sure he's after our money. It has been more than a week since your father's death and he has been practically living here throughout that time. He obviously doesn't have any work to do. We'd better be wary of him."

Rana wasn't offended when Arjun glared at him. The boy was too young and immature to understand the ways of the world.

He was surprised when he felt Arjun's firm hand on his shoulder. "Rana Uncle, please do me a favour. You can see that we are going to be extremely busy over the next few weeks. The police will probably want to interrogate me as well. Why don't you and the others get back to your regular lives? It's bound to get more traumatic for Grandpa and Grandma too. They are better off staying away from the scene."

Rana's lips moved but no sound came from his mouth. He had never expected young Arjun to talk like this. Was he really asking them to get out? He turned to look at Smita, Nandita and Deo. They appeared ashamed as they nodded their heads in unison and left to pack their bags without uttering a word.

What now? All his attempts to gain a part of Jayant Mathur's wealth appeared to be going down the drain. He turned to appeal to Jayant's son, "Listen Arjun. You are too young to handle all this by yourself. You will need our support. If Deo has work, let him go. But I have a lot of leave. Let me..."

Arjun smiled at him. "Thank you, Rana Uncle. Why don't you save your leave for the time when Ritu gets married? It will be of better use then. Allow me to manage my own business."

Left with no choice, an angry Rana left the Mathur home. But that didn't stop him from spouting abuse about Anjali and Bhardwaj to the press waiting outside the building. His temper improved the more he spoke to the media, thrilled to be the centre of attention for a change.

13

rjun was livid as he watched his relatives leave. He touched the feet of his Grandpa and Grandma before hugging them. "Sorry Grandpa, but this is for the best. This is only going to get uglier. I'll keep you posted about further developments."

"You are a brave boy, Arjun. Do not worry. It's a terrible tragedy that your father was murdered. I don't understand who would have wanted to see him dead. He was such a great soul," said Grandpa, wiping his eyes. "You take care—of yourself and your mother. That Parth Bhardwaj is truly an exceptional friend. I don't know how we could have all managed without him over the past few days."

Arjun nodded, valiantly holding back his tears. He shut the door behind everyone to go sit on the sofa to cool his temper. Rana Uncle was so mean. He was worried about "our money" indeed. He had noticed that Rana had been unhappy to take a backseat when Parth was running around and doing everything. But then, Rana wasn't the kind of person one could trust. He was glad that Grandpa at least recognised Parth's worth.

A deep sigh broke out from Arjun. The police had begun their interrogation with his mother and Parth. But that wasn't going to help them find the murderer.

His father's gun had been found short of one bullet and the police had managed to verify that the missing bullet was the one which had been lodged in Jayant's chest. But who had done the actual shooting? There were no fingerprints on the gun. None! Not even Jayant's own, considering the weapon had belonged to him. It had been wiped thoroughly clean.

Could the murder have been planned in advance then? In that case, the murderer must have known that his father kept a gun in his bedside drawer. Then, obviously, the killer couldn't be a stranger.

Arjun wanted to howl in frustration. Who would have wanted his father dead? And why? It looked like unless the murderer came forth and confessed to his guilt, there was no way to trace the person.

14

I t was Inspector Phadke who did the questioning, speaking to Anjali Mathur first while the DCP sat back, listening keenly. "You have mentioned that at the time of Mr Jayant Mathur's murder, you were sleeping in a separate bedroom."

"Yes. I moved into the guest bedroom a couple of months ago," she replied softly.

Hmm... she was ready to share more information than he asked. Phadke nodded to himself before continuing, "How long have you been married to Mr Mathur?"

"A little more than twenty years."

"Was there a specific reason for you to move into a separate room?" Phadke was kind of embarrassed, asking this question. Though it was part of the routine, he was still not hardened enough to be completely insensitive.

"I moved out and later filed for a divorce."

Phadke was surprised. Their preliminary investigations had not brought that up. He made a note to acquire a copy of the official divorce papers from the concerned court. "And when was that Mrs Mathur? I mean, when did you file for divorce?"

"Almost two months ago. And both Jayant and I had agreed on it. It was mutual," her voice was devoid of emotion.

"Then how come both of you were still living in the same house?"

"We had our reasons, Inspector Phadke, those that I regret terribly. You know how it is in high society. Jayant wanted to get some things in order before we announced to the public that we were going separate."

Phadke had a few more routine questions before he excused himself to talk to Parth Bhardwaj. "Hello Mr Bhardwaj. I see that you are a friend of the Mathur family. Can you tell me whose friend you actually are?"

"I'm a friend of both Anjali and Arjun Mathur."

"Have you known the Mathurs for long?"

A small frown of concentration appeared on Parth's face as he seemed to calculate furiously. "Must be around six months, I think."

Phadke thought of asking about Bhardwaj's relationship with Anjali Mathur. But then, he had heard from many different sources that they were close, and the question served no purpose just now.

"What do you do for a living?" It was routine, for the sake of record. Phadke knew the answer.

"I'm a full-time author. I write thrillers and travelogues."

"How well did you know Mr Jayant Mathur?"

"Not all that well. I have met him a few times. We didn't have much in common."

"But you covet his wife," said Phadke, throwing a punch in the dark. This was getting very frustrating. Both of them appeared too straightforward; not bothered about hiding their relationship. If that's how it was, he couldn't think of a motive for their killing Jayant Mathur. Of course, he still needed proof of a divorce filed. But from what he could see so far, Mathur had more reason to kill these two than the other way round.

Parth smiled. "'Covet' is a strong word, Inspector Phadke. One can covet something which belongs to someone else. Anjali did not belong to Jayant Mathur when I met her. She had already mentally moved far away from him."

That sounded logical, even if it didn't throw any light on the situation. More than anything, Parth's statement matched with everything Anjali Mathur had herself stated. Only, Phadke found himself at a dead end, unable to understand the cause of Jayant Mathur's murder. It was time to move away from the family and begin his search at Mathur's place of work and his friend circle.

15

About six months ago...

Anjali turned around to look at her sleeping husband. Even after being married to him for the last twenty years, she was fascinated by the way he snored away just a couple of minutes after the event... as if... as if he was absolutely satisfied with a duty well done.

She scrunched up her nose in distaste. She was not sure she understood the male species at all. She walked towards the bathroom, a bed-sheet wrapped around her otherwise naked body. Yes, even after living with the man for almost two decades, she wasn't comfortable walking around in the nude, especially considering that the said man was fast asleep.

Anjali closed the door to the bathroom quietly before pulling the sheet from her body. The tube-light above the full-length mirror reflected her glorious body without the camouflage of civilisation, same as the day she was born.

She looked at her body critically, a small frown puckering her dark eyebrows. She was almost thirty-nine, having married when she was barely nineteen, while her only son was that age now.

Not bad, she thought, not bad at all. Her face was smooth, not a wrinkle in sight. Her skin was the colour of golden wheat, a tiny dark mole above the left side of her upper lip. Her nose was slim and straight, her lips—the upper one thin while the lower one sensuously lush. Her cheeks were shining with health, a bit on the chubbier side.

Finally, Anjali's eyes moved to their reflection in the mirror. The dark brown eyes mirrored the sadness she felt within. They were framed by long lashes which were slightly damp from the sheen of tears which had inadvertently appeared in them.

"Tch." Anjali rubbed an impatient hand over her eyes and shook her head to herself before her gaze moved further down. Her neck was slim while her shoulders were narrow. She skimmed over her breasts before moving further down until her gaze reached her toes. She had never enjoyed sex with Jayant, not that she had known it with any other man. She knew that many people called the act 'making love', but she couldn't relate to that.

Her lips took a downward curve. Was sex exciting? She knew not. Jayant and Anjali had sex whenever he felt like it, which was may be two or three times in a month. Was it because they had become habits to each other? But then, the pattern had been kind of the same from the inception of their marriage.

Anjali had no close friends. She was a rich businessman's wife and hence had to hold herself aloof. Otherwise, hubby dear wouldn't approve. Early on in their marriage, her parents-in-law had set stringent rules on her comings and goings. She had given in, as she also was from a conservative family.

Just when she had started baulking at the restrictions, Jayant had decided to set up a separate household for them, more for his convenience than out of consideration for his wife. He had become an excellent businessman by then while all the wheeling and dealing were done at the parties he hosted. Old-fashioned parents were getting in the way and hence the plan to go separate.

It only made Anjali wonder whether she had fallen out of the frying pan into the fire. She gave her long, slim legs a cursory glance in the mirror before getting into the shower cubicle and turning on the spray. She was five feet, five inches tall and weighed fifty-eight kilos. She did yoga and meditation for about two hours every day. She was happy most of the time. Only on such nights, when she felt her husband insult her femininity, that she wondered about her aimless existence.

Wham, bam and not even a thank you ma'am were the words which came to her mind. But then she was his wife, not a favoured girlfriend. A wife was as good as a doormat, she thought. Her blood sizzled despite the chillness of the shower. Why was she putting up with this?

Anjali ran the towel mechanically over her aroused body, careful not to touch herself. She thought of the two lady characters in the film *Fire*; how they turn lesbians, driven by the negligence of their respective husbands. She shook her head while pulling out the hairpins holding up her jet-black hair as it cascaded in a silken curtain down to her waist. The strands crackled with electricity as she combed her scalp with her fingers. Though she felt driven, she couldn't imagine seeking another woman's body.

No! She needed a man.

Her shocked eyes found their reflection in the mirror. Oh my God! What was she thinking of? No! She was married into a respectable family. Her husband was a rich and successful businessman. She was short of nothing in life. She had a wardrobe full of clothes, a locker full of jewellery in the latest designs, several bank accounts which overflowed with money, credit cards galore. They lived in a luxurious apartment with four bedrooms. They had three servants at their beck and call and a cook to boot. What more could she ask for?

A loving husband? A man who would hug her spontaneously? One who would give her five minutes of his undivided attention? Anjali's mind screamed in response. These were things which all her money couldn't buy.

Anjali drew her nightie of superfine cotton over her slender body and stepped out of the bathroom. She could see her husband sprawled over three-fourths of their bed and a sigh shook her body. Not one night had she slept in his arms! She moved towards the bed before stopping midstride. No, she didn't want to sleep near her unresponsive husband. She walked to the adjoining dressing room, a pillow and sheet clutched in her hand. She switched on the air-conditioner there, curled up on the couch and whiled the night away, wide awake.

16

rjun was excited. Jane and he had just moved into a two-bedroom apartment close to the university campus. He had met her for the first time three months ago when he joined Kingston University, London.

He had felt attracted to her from the moment he looked into her emerald green eyes. With a pixie face, honey blonde hair and wide lips which always smiled, Jane had caught his attention from the word go.

After all those hours together at the college library and coffee shops, they were getting frustrated each time they had to say 'goodbye' and go back to their respective rooms in the hostel. That was when they decided to move in together.

Jane McKenzie was from Scotland and had won a scholarship to Kingston. She was majoring in English literature. Though she wasn't happy about Arjun paying the rent, he had been adamant. He had money to burn while she worked as a waitress at a local restaurant for a few hours every day. She was fiercely independent and had refused to give up her job. Arjun respected her all the more for it.

Arjun planned to call his mother that day and talk to her about his move. Though they were mother and son, Anjali and Arjun were friends first. He could talk to her freely as she had an open mind. He adored her.

He loved his father too, but their relationship was different. Jayant was a typical father and a bit on the conservative side. He also spoilt his only son rotten. Not that Arjun objected to it. But his mother was the one who maintained the balance in their family of three.

He knew that his mother must be missing him terribly. Not that she would ever have stopped him from going ahead with his life. But she led such a restricted life. He knew how she hated her life of leisure. While there must be so many women out there envying her, Arjun knew how much his mother resented being idle. With a sharp mind, she loved to be in action. Till six months ago, Arjun had been the centre of her existence. With him living so far away, it wouldn't be easy for her. He really needed to find a way to keep her busy, without his father getting upset about it. It wouldn't be easy, but not impossible.

17

"Anjali!" A yell ripped into her disturbed sleep, jerking her awake. She looked at the clock. 7.30. She had finally drifted off to sleep barely an hour ago. She got up wearily and walked to the bedroom as Jayant shouted again, "Anjali, where the hell are you?"

She stifled a yawn as she opened the connecting door, calling out, "Coming."

"It's high time, your highness. Some of us have work to do. I have to be in the office by 8.30 if you want to lead the life of a lady of leisure. Would it be too much to expect that you can arrange for my clothes to be available to me every morning, especially considering that you have four servants to order about while sitting on your butt?" greeted her husband.

Anjali didn't reply as she went to his wardrobe to pick out his clothes for the day. He had been standing there with a towel around his waist, arms akimbo, yelling at the top of his voice, without even bothering to find out if everything was there. But then, he had been spoilt rotten from childhood, by his mother and two older sisters, him being the only pampered male child.

Every time Jayant's voice rose in anger, which was often, Anjali withdrew more into her shell. She felt stripped of her self-respect. She felt terribly hurt by the way Jayant treated her, like a dumb woman, a doormat to be precise. Sometimes, Anjali found her very existence suffocating, not having a clue about how to escape from it.

The one saving grace in the mess of Anjali's life was their son. She smiled to herself when she thought of Arjun. He had been a little more than eighteen when he left home to live and study in England. Arjun was cheerful as opposed to his father's grumpy nature. He was fun to be with and had been the centre of Anjali's universe. It was more than six months now since Arjun left home and Anjali felt as if she lived in a mausoleum nowadays.

She left the bedroom after ensuring Jayant had all that he needed. She closed the bathroom door behind her and leaned against it with a sigh. She had the whole day stretching out in front of her and she couldn't think of one interesting thing to do.

She brushed her teeth and washed before getting out, to find Jayant standing in front of the mirror fixing his tie. She ignored him as she opened her wardrobe to remove a new set of *salwar kameez* in a bright canary yellow patterned in blood red and turquoise blue. She needed the bright colours to cheer her up.

Sometimes she wondered at herself. What was she living for? What was it that made her move from one day to the next? Frankly, there was nothing to motivate her. Not a thing to look forward to. She didn't notice Jayant's eyes following her every movement like a hawk.

"So which kitty party are you off to, today?" barked Jayant in a rough voice, his dark eyes glittering in anger.

"None, if it's any of your business," came the quick retort.

Jayant leapt across the room in two strides and placing a rough hand on her shoulder, turned Anjali around to face him. "Don't you dare turn your back on me, woman," he snarled, his eyes red with temper. "And learn to show some respect for me. I'm your husband who also pays all your bills."

Anjali's lips curled in obvious disgust. "Are you sure that's what you are? The way you talk, anybody would think you are an elderly relative and not my life partner."

The barb hit home. Jayant clenched his fists in frustration, turned on his heel and walked out of the bedroom without uttering a word.

A silent Anjali dressed quickly and went into the dining room where Jayant was eating a hearty breakfast. She poured herself a cup of coffee and sat at the opposite end of the table, as far away from her husband as possible.

"We've been invited to the Vermas' place for a party tonight. Be ready by 7.30. I will either pick you up or send the car and driver. We've to be there early," Jayant told Anjali.

Anjali nodded her head desultorily, her lips drooping. She was fed up with the meaningless parties which she had been attending over the years at her husband's side. The drinking, the forceful laughter and the whole false nature of these affairs grated on her nerves. Oh, what was the use?!

18

J ayant got into the luxurious back seat of his Black Mercedes and told his driver, "Office *chalo*!" before getting immersed in the documents he removed from his leather briefcase.

He was five feet, ten inches tall and maintained himself well, except for the small paunch thanks to the amount of alcohol he imbibed. He was forty-six and had a few grey hairs at his temples which added to the looks of a dashing businessman. He was the life and soul of every party he hosted or attended and the women adored him. And he loved them too!

Jayant didn't understand his wife Anjali at all. He found her cold and was never sure how to talk to her. He felt that whatever he told her—once the words left his lips—sounded wrong. It only made him angry and impatient with her. He had given her so much—the luxurious life of a lotus-eater. Why the hell wasn't she happy? It was obvious to him that she wasn't, though he couldn't understand why. It never struck him to simply ask her.

Jayant was convinced that he was married to a shrew. In the beginning, she had seemed like an innocent and life was hunky dory when they lived with his parents. She had been a polite daughter-in-law and her claws had never showed. After they moved separately—she had been twenty-four then—he got to see her true colours. She was stubborn and did what she pleased. And over and above, she had no qualms about talking back to her wonderful husband. Jayant couldn't condone a woman talking back to a man. Yes, he did live in the eighteenth century that way.

He preferred to be in control, whether it was his business or his household. He adopted the most modern of methods in his business and ran it up-to-date befitting the new millennium. Jayant made it a point to attend many online courses and updated himself on the various methods used internationally in similar businesses.

But there was no school for domesticity. Whatever he knew, he applied from what he had learned as a child. He had been pampered because he was a male. His parents had treated him like a divine being who walked the earth while his sisters—though elder to him—had always had to take a backseat. He got the best food, best clothes, best education, best treatment, and maximum love, because he was a man.

Why the hell couldn't his wife continue to treat him in the same fashion? Anjali would never be able to survive without him. And shouldn't she be grateful for having such a good-looking, successful businessman for a husband? He showered her with money, with luxury. He knew of a dozen women at least who would give their right arm to be in Anjali's place. But did she appreciate that?

He didn't know how to handle her. They had no common ground. She was never interested in anything he wanted to do. She wanted to read and browse the net. Even when they travelled, he enjoyed socialising and chilling in the luxurious hotel suite. While she wanted to run around, seeing the sights. What the hell was there to see? If you have seen one country, you have seen them all.

Jayant felt annoyed. Like today, when he needed to get to work early, the Queen Bee had been fast asleep. Shouldn't she have been up and gotten everything ready for him? Wasn't it a wife's duty to take care of her husband? And it wasn't as if she was a career woman who spent a large part of her day at work.

At times, he had to hold himself back from slapping her. Not because he was chivalrous. It was because he knew for a fact that his wife would just hit him right back. He had his pride too.

Jayant forced himself to relax and thought of the party they were to attend that evening. At least, his wife was a great asset there. She was welcomed in all homes, which in turn helped smoothen his way around his business connections. Even as a hostess, he couldn't find any fault with her. *I suppose she has her advantages,* sighed Jayant to himself as his car entered the building where he had his offices.

19

Anjali sat in front of the TV after Jayant left. Sita, the cook, came out to check with the lunch menu. Anjali gave her the instructions in a desultory fashion. Once that was done, she surfed channels. There was nothing which caught her fancy.

She went into her room to pick up her favourite thriller by Paul Bainsbridge. Her lips turned down as she ran her eyes through the book-shelf. She had read all his six books only last month—for the second time. She didn't feel like reading them again, not so soon. She thought of clearing out her wardrobe and re-arranging her clothes. But then, she had done that only last week.

The phone rang just as she was about to step out of her room. She went back and picked up the hand-set next to the bed and said, "Hello!"

"Hey Mom! It's me, Arjun," came her son's voice over the line.

"Arjun," squealed his mother in delight. "How are you, my dear?"

"Just awesome, Mom. And you? How are you?"

"I'm okay," she replied unenthusiastically. "So, tell me. Have you settled down to the English way of life? How do you like the food there? How are your roommates? Do you cook at all? And..."

"Whoa, Mommy dear, easy," laughed Arjun. Anjali could just picture him laughing and an answering grin tugged at her lips. "I called to say I've shifted. Actually Mom, I'm..."

"You've found a girl," declared his mother.

"Mom!" Arjun's voice was startled.

"Oh! Did I get that wrong?" she asked, pretty sure about her guess.

"Well, Mom! You're kinda right. I..."

"What do you mean, kinda? You are either in a relationship or you aren't," She replied in her typical forthright way.

"Well, actually, we just moved into the new apartment. Jane and I thought of setting up house together and see how things work. Whether we are compatible and all that, you know."

"You mean you haven't made love?" asked Anjali.

Trust his mother to get to the core of the issue. "Mom, I wonder what I'd do without you. That's why I called. We took the decision and we are together, just from today morning. Now I've cold feet." The son was no less frank than the mother. But then, that was the kind of relationship they shared. They could openly discuss anything under the sun. Also, Anjali had consciously taught Arjun to be sensitive to a woman's needs unlike his own father.

"I just wanted to ask you if I am doing the right thing."

"What do you feel for Jane? Do you feel a strong sense of chemistry or is it something more than that?" came the blunt query.

"I find her totally attractive, Mom," replied Arjun.

"She doesn't believe that this might last forever, does she? I mean, you haven't given her any false impression, right? Don't make her any promise which you don't intend keeping. It's better to take it a day at a time and just have fun. Live life happily," advised Anjali.

Arjun's voice was choked as he replied, "You're simply awesome, Mom. I love you so much. And Mom, thank you."

"Hey, you're welcome anytime. Giving advice is easy and also comes free," her voice cracked over the last sentence.

"Are you okay Mom? Do you want me to come home?" There was a trace of anxiety in Arjun's voice.

"Don't be silly dear. Of course not. You carry on. I'm quite fine. It's the usual. You know how it is," Anjali pacified him.

"Mom, why don't you just leave Dad and make a life for yourself?" asked her son.

Anjali was shocked. She gasped, "Arjun, what are you saying? Have you gone mad?" She couldn't think of living life differently.

"No, Mom! I'm serious. You both are so different from each other. He's a focused businessman and both of us know that his work consumes him. And he takes pride in it. But you... you Mom, have built your life around him, your every action is just a reaction to his. But then again, you're an individual, a thinker at that. You think modern, you're broadminded, creative and a go-getter. Your life is wasted at home. Why not just get out?"

Anjali shook her head in disbelief. Out of the mouths of babes! Her son had grown up and how! He had put together the set-up of her life or rather the lack of it in just a few sentences. She was astounded.

"Mom, are you still there?"

"Of course, Arjun. I'm just speechless with wonder."

"Well... a suggestion. Why don't you come over here and spend time with me? You'll find loads to do. There's a gym, yoga centre, library and even a temple nearby. You can go for long walks. You can..."

"Easy!" laughed Anjali. "No Arjun. Not so soon. You've just gone to live by yourself. You settle down and enjoy your independence. I don't want to step into your space. And then again, do you want me to play gooseberry between you and Jane?" she teased.

"Mom, you're just impossible and right, as always. It's just..."

"Smart are the kids who realise that their moms are always right," quipped his mother.

"Just be happy," continued Arjun. "So, what are you doing today?"

"The usual. Going to a party in the evening. Husband's orders! I'm bored sick of the whole scene," she cribbed.

"Hey Mom! Deck yourself in a beautiful sari, maybe a brilliant orange one. Wear some lovely matching jewellery. In fact, why don't you go to your beautician and get gorgeous? And knock them out for a six. Will you do it for me, please?"

His enthusiasm caught on. "I like the idea," said Anjali. "Yes!" she snapped her fingers, "You're perfect, sonny. I'll get an oil massage from head to toe along with a facial, manicure and pedicure. You made my day, love you." There was a smile in Anjali's voice.

"Love you too, Mom. Have a great time. Will call you tomorrow to check, for sure. Do send me a selfie once you are all decked up. Will introduce you to Jane too," said Arjun.

"Sure Arjun. You take care and do send me a picture of you and Jane together. Keep her happy. Have a great time!" She blew him a kiss as she put the receiver down, her step more purposeful now.

20

Parth stared at the screen of his laptop blankly and shook his head in disgust. He got up for the fifth time in two hours to make himself a cup of coffee. His mind ran over the lines he had written from morning. Yeah, lines. He should have completed at least one whole chapter by now. He looked at the wall clock in the kitchen. It was 5.30 pm. He had been at the keyboard from eight in the morning. And what had he got to show for it? Zilch! Good for him that he had taught himself to type directly on to a Word document. A few years back, he would have torn up sheets of paper to fill half a dozen waste paper baskets at the rate at which he had typed and erased today.

He stretched his long arms towards the ceiling as the milk came to a boil on the stove. Parth realised that he was hungry. He had skipped lunch. He opened the freezer to check out the contents. There was one pizza left from the batch he had made last week. He removed it and placed it in the microwave and set it to 'defrost'.

He picked up the mug of coffee he had made and walked out of the French windows to the huge balcony. He lived in the penthouse on the thirty-fifth floor of *Olympus*, the building a part of the high-end Hiranandani Gardens in Powai. His apartment took up the whole floor, giving him the privacy he sought. The setting sun made his face glow with health. Parth's eyes appeared like molten silver in the sun's golden rays. The said rays highlighted the few silver strands woven into his teak brown curls which grew down to cover his nape.

Parth was handsome in a rugged way, his features portraying a sharp intelligence and worldly wisdom which he had acquired over the forty-two years of his life. He had run away from home as a kid and never bothered to complete his formal education, convinced that the experience he gained travelling the globe as more than sufficient.

Even as he worked hard on the ships which took him around the world, Parth read every scrap of paper which came his way—newspapers, magazines, books, just about everything. By stint of hard work and discipline, Parth proved his mettle by amassing wealth over the years, saving his hard-earned money and making the right investments. Now he was so wealthy that he could help his nieces and nephews with their education, he could support his parents—which he had been doing right from the day he began to earn; he owned three different properties in and around Mumbai and had a finger each in many different corporate pies.

All this wealth had helped him settle down to what he had always wanted to do—write. He already had six bestselling thrillers and a travelogue on Finland to his name. Right now, Parth was simultaneously writing a travelogue on Africa and another thriller. His agent had found him a new publisher for both. The travelogue could wait. But the thriller was due to be turned in within the month.

Parth's wide chest rose in a deep sigh. It startled him with its unexpectedness. What the fuck! He was stuck three-fourths of the way into his novel by a major writer's block. He couldn't seem to put pen to paper. In this case, fingers to keyboard. If he didn't deliver, his reputation would be at stake.

Ramakant, his agent, had called him last night to remind him of his deadline. But what did an agent know about creative juices which got temperamental? The ebb and flow were not in his hands. Parth felt cornered and didn't like it at all. All the hard work over the years to become his own master seemed not worth it now. He was again a slave to his agent and publisher.

A heavy frown drew Parth's dark eyebrows together. How to break through this maze he seemed to be stuck in? He didn't feel inclined to sit at his laptop again, not today. He went to the microwave to heat the pizza for a few minutes before transferring it to a plate and slicing it up. Taking it to the dining table on the other side of the kitchen, he straddled a chair and munched away at the pieces, not really tasting them. His mind was busy chewing the problem he was having with his story.

He realised that he needed to get away. He should mingle with other human beings. He hadn't met a soul other than his maid servant over the past five days. He jogged in the middle of the night to avoid people. Parth opened his iPhone to refer to his calendar to check on upcoming events which he could attend. He ran his finger down the list to reach March 24—a party at the Vermas. He recalled Ranjit and Ruchika Vermas' faces instantaneously and with startling clarity. But then, Parth had a photographic memory which stored a horde of information he could draw upon at will, with absolute precision.

The couple were in their mid-forties and obviously fun-loving. The lady had a horsey laugh and a tendency to cling. For whatever reason, she seemed to be under the impression that Parth was free and available. She refused to accept the fact that he steered clear of married women.

Today was their wedding anniversary party. Did he dare go?

A smile lit up Parth's features as he shrugged his shoulders. What did he stand to lose? Right now, he needed to get away from his home and a wild party seemed to be the perfect antidote for his blues.

It was seven. The party began at 7.30 and was taking place at the Vermas' home just a few buildings away in the same campus. He decided to live it up that evening.

21

njali was waiting in the living room of her flat when driver Ramu came to pick her up that evening. No one would have recognised the irritated woman from morning. She had taken Arjun's advice to heart and gone to her beautician for the day. The result was a glowing Anjali, appearing not a day over thirty.

Her hair fell down to the middle of her back in a dark silken curtain with subtle gold highlights. Her face glowed with minimal make-up and a touch of deep mauve lipstick. She wore a pure crepe sari of mauve that had embroidered rose-bud motifs in gold *zari*. Amethysts and diamonds winked at her neck, ears, wrists and finger.

She got into the car and took the five-minute ride to the building where the Vermas lived. It was a distance she could have walked easily. But then, what would have happened to her husband's reputation? Anjali refused to get angry. She was feeling too nice just now.

The Vermas occupied the whole of the first and second floors of their building. The party was on a lavish scale and the crowd overflowed into the gorgeous terrace garden on the lower level.

"Hello Anjali, welcome, welcome," gushed Ranjit as he took her hand in both of his. Anjali controlled the feeling of revulsion she felt at his touch. She greeted him with a smile that didn't quite reach her eyes and wished him a great wedding anniversary. Her eyes searched for Ruchika as she heard her hostess's distinct laugh to the left.

Anjali extricated her hand from Ranjit's and walked to Ruchika. "Hello Anjali," shrilled Ruchika, "I'm so glad that you could make it to our little celebration." She opened her arms wide and Anjali had no choice but to hug her. She air-kissed Ruchika before offering her best wishes.

"Oh, thank you my dear. Jayant's already here. But then, he's a darling. Always there for us. He's..." Anjali tuned out of the chatter as she noticed her husband in the throng of admirers who had been surrounding Ruchika.

When the driver had come to pick her up, Anjali had been under the impression that Jayant had been delayed at work. But it was obvious that he had got off at the Verma residence and sent the car for her. Anjali wondered whether it made any sense to feel hurt. This wasn't the first time he had treated her in such a callous fashion. Shouldn't she be used to it after all these years?

But she couldn't stop the feeling of betrayal which washed over her. And who was that standing a couple of steps away from Jayant? Anjali was surprised—no, shocked—to see Seema, Jayant's executive assistant. What was that woman doing here? She swallowed her questions and picked up a full glass from the tray held by a passing waiter, not even bothering to check what it contained.

Anjali walked to the side of the room, trying to find an empty seat. When she couldn't, she leaned against a wall and turned around to watch the drama unfolding in front of her. She nodded and smiled at acquaintances while Jayant ignored her completely.

Anjali turned pale when she saw her husband holding his secretary too close to his body. She also noticed Seema squirming when she caught Anjali's eye.

Feeling bitter, Anjali took a sip from her glass and gagged. It was some kind of a cocktail containing vodka, gin and what else, she didn't know. She never drank anything stronger than wine, that too rarely. What was she doing with the glass? She hailed a passing waiter and gave it to him. She had spent the whole day dolling herself up for what—to watch her husband holding his secretary like a delicate china doll? Anger made Anjali's face red.

Though Anjali found an empty chair and sat on it for a brief while, she couldn't stop her eyes from straying to Jayant and Seema who appeared to be glued to each other. She got up suddenly and walked up the staircase to the first floor, needing to get as far away as possible from her husband and his latest mistress.

S eema paled the moment she saw Anjali enter the Vermas' home. She had accompanied her boss Jayant to the party, believing that it was going to be just the two of them. How could he do this to her, to both of them actually? She picked up a glass of Scotch-on-the-rocks and drank it at one go. Her hand shook as she placed the empty glass on a tray nearby. Over and above that, Seema felt threatened by Anjali's classy looks. She felt so dowdy in comparison. Her neat black trouser-suit had been perfect for work. Though she had changed into a fresh, pale pink frilly blouse, it was nowhere as resplendent as Anjali's silk sari and precious jewellery. Seema felt bereft.

She refused to look at Jayant as he crushed her to his side. Was he trying to underline the point that she was his arm candy and nothing more? Seema hated herself at that moment.

Being a thirty-seven-year-old career woman had both its pluses and minuses. She had been so focussed on climbing up her professional ladder that she had given up on the small joys of living a personal life. She had worked hard from the level of a lowly clerk to the position of executive assistant to the big boss. Not once had she compromised on her dignity.

But now, with Jayant paying her so much attention, she had given in to temptation, when he wooed her day in and day out.

He had pleaded with her, cajoled her. He flirted with her and bought her gifts—both expensive and inexpensive trinkets. All these years, Seema had never thought of getting married or even having an affair. This was the first time a man was showing so much interest in her. He wooed her over five months.

"Yes, I'm married. But that doesn't mean I live a happy life. You don't know my wife. She's a shrew. There are days when I hate going home." A man shouldn't look so attractive despite the sad eyes and droopy lips. Seema's heart melted. Jayant needed to be loved. And she had no one. She never stopped to think beyond that before becoming his sweetheart.

She shut her ears to all the gossip about his numerous affairs. What if he had been searching for a woman to love him all these years? Poor man! Love couldn't have been blinder and deafer than Seema's. She fell into his arms, hook, line and sinker.

Today, coming face to face with Anjali, Seema was shocked out of her wits. The woman was hauntingly beautiful. How could Jayant want to sleep with Seema while having Anjali for his wife?

The evening had lost its charm.

23

Jayant's arm went around Seema defiantly. He had decided he would show that selfish wife of his who was superior. All these days, he had been discreet with his affairs. But today morning, Anjali's behaviour had exceeded all boundaries. Now, he planned to flaunt his girlfriends in public. Let her feel ashamed. As for himself, Jayant knew that society's rules were less stringent for men. Anyway, what he was doing was nothing uncommon in the high society they belonged to. He saw that Anjali had settled into a chair in a corner of the room and turned to catch the eye of their hostess Ruchika with a smirk on his face.

Now there was a woman he truly admired. There was nothing Ruchika wouldn't do for Ranjit. The two were a fabulous pair. Whether it was hosting parties or arranging picnics or just pleasing any of Ranjit's friends—Ruchika jumped into everything with an enthusiasm which Jayant envied. He wished Anjali would be more like her.

And then there was Seema. His executive assistant was a tigress in bed. He would never have guessed it by her quiet demeanour. He wasn't clear what had attracted him to her in the first place. What had truly surprised him was her being a virgin at that age. A small part of Jayant felt proud that he was her first lover.

Now, why couldn't his wife Anjali be more like one of these women? She was no fun at all. While she organised great parties and seemed to keep everyone entertained, she always seemed remote, as if she disapproved the whole party scene. He couldn't quite understand what made her tick. But then, Jayant had never asked her about it. It didn't strike him to hold a meaningful conversation with Anjali, not once from the time they got married two decades ago.

Never for a second did Jayant feel guilty about his extra-marital affairs. All men did it, especially those as successful as he was. His favourite dialogue was, "Even our forefathers had such a lifestyle. What about all those kings and their harems? Polygamy has always been a part of civilised society. It was only much later that the Hindu Law banned men from taking more than a single wife."

He was clear that his wife had no right to question his activities. Well, he did provide for her, didn't he? She should be thrilled with her life of leisure. He couldn't fathom why she didn't seem all that happy with her life. But then, she was an ungrateful bitch. That's what she was!

Having arrived at that conclusion, Jayant shrugged his shoulders and decided to forget his wife for the rest of the evening.

24

The many expressions chasing Anjali's face fascinated the man entering the front door. He was twenty minutes late. As if he cared! But his hostess pounced on him the moment he stepped in and shrieked, "Parth darling, you made it despite your busy schedule. That's so awesome! And thank you darling, for your lovely wishes," she continued as he gave her the elaborate bouquet of flowers. "How are you? Do come in and meet everyone." She dragged him into the split-level hall and started introducing all the friends and neighbours who had come for the party.

Parth didn't know anyone other than the Vermas as it was only recently that he had moved into the colony.

Ruchika clapped her hands. "Listen peeps! This is Parth Bhardwaj. He's a writer who lives up there on his Mount Olympus," she laughed at her own joke before continuing, "Today he has climbed down his mountain to grace our wedding anniversary. He..." She droned on, unaware that she had lost her eminent guest's attention.

He obviously made the right noises whenever she paused and looked towards him, but Parth's eyes were trained on the woman in mauve. There was such an air of melancholy surrounding her that it hit Parth powerfully. Did no one else notice her? She was sitting all by herself, looking gorgeous and lost—like an oasis in the middle of a desert.

Parth tried his best to move in her direction. But he was surrounded by too many people demanding his attention. He hailed a passing waiter and got himself a glass of Scotch-on-the-rocks. He swirled the ice cubes as he listened to Ranjit Verma extolling the virtues of the latest murder mystery he had read. Every now and again, he looked up to check that the woman in mauve was still seated in her corner. He willed that the guests' focus shift away from him so that he could approach her.

The DJ began playing some popular tunes and the crowd moved away to the space set aside for dancing. Free from the attention of the other guests, Parth moved in the direction of that lovely woman only to see the tail end of her sari flash around the bend in the staircase. He picked up a second glass of Scotch and walked leisurely up the stairs, determined to make her acquaintance.

It was fifteen minutes and quite a search of the whole of the second floor of the Vermas' flat before Parth located his quarry. He saw her standing alone in a small balcony off a side bedroom. She was doubled up, hugging herself, her head bent low, as if in pain.

Not stopping to think, Parth walked up to her. Unable to see her anguish, he put both his arms around her from behind and hugged her close, his chin pressed to the top of her head. His hug was platonic, from one human being to another, offering solace.

25

I t wasn't easy to hold back her tears, which was why Anjali decided to go away to the upper floor of the duplex, away from the revelry. Yes, she was aware of her husband's many affairs. She had chosen to bury her head in the sand as long as they didn't intrude on her life. She and Jayant obviously never discussed it. And the people they knew in common never dared to mention it. Despite being an open secret, Anjali had somehow managed to convince herself that everything was well with her marriage.

But today, Jayant had dared to invite his arm candy to the same party as his wife. This was not done, not even in the elite society they lived in. Anjali was sure that she must be a laughing stock by now. How dare he shame her like this? The guests at the party were all well known to both of them. How the hell could he bring his latest mistress to this party?

Finding an empty bedroom, Anjali walked out to the balcony attached to it and stood there, holding the railing so tightly that her fingers hurt, not that she was aware of the pain. She looked down blindly at the garden. Luckily, it was the back of the building and there were no guests there. She stared down at the lawn, her eyes unseeing, her shoulders slumped in pain, willing her tears to go away.

What was the use of crying? It was only her fault that her life was in such a mess. What had she been doing all these years, leading the life of a housewife? Why the hell hadn't she created a career for herself? Life wasn't only about bringing up a child and waiting on one's husband hand and foot. While the child had grown up and flown the nest, the husband obviously didn't care for her. Was there a point to such an existence?

Instead of drying up, the tears poured faster. Though she didn't like the idea of blaming someone for her sorry existence, Anjali couldn't help recalling the many times she had tried to do something with her life, only to have her husband raise an objection, every time.

There was a time when Anjali wanted to learn music. She bought herself a keyboard and booked herself into a class which ran for a couple of hours, thrice a week. The first two weeks had passed in excitement as she learned the notes of three different Bollywood numbers, all her favourites.

She walked out of the class that Wednesday and sat in the car to check her phone. There were eight missed calls from Jayant. Not highly perturbed, Anjali called him back. He was always in a rush and she was sure it was no emergency. "Hello Jayant..."

"Why the hell didn't you take my calls? And you are obviously out," he roared. He must have of course called their home too. "What's so important that you don't take my calls?" If anything, his voice became louder.

"But Jayant, I told you that I'm going to a music class..."

"What? Music?" he laughed sarcastically. "What does Aurangzeb know about music? Your place is at home, taking care of Arjun and me. Stop going to the class, NOW. Do you hear me?"

She was sure the whole of his office must have heard him. Anjali felt terribly hurt, but she knew her husband. If he said 'no', he meant 'no'. He would never let her be in peace until she listened to him. Might as well stop the class now instead of later when he became impossible to deal with.

From that afternoon, the keyboard was locked away in the back of her wardrobe, never to see the light of day again.

Anjali felt like a bird with clipped wings. Her husband trimmed them regularly, ensuring that she never was free to do things on her own.

Just now, all those instances came to the fore and she was too upset with her life. As Anjali fought with her emotions, she was startled to feel a pair of arms going around her, hugging her close to a masculine frame.

She shuddered as strange sensations bombarded her. The arms holding her were hard and muscular while their grip was so gentle. Could such a thing be possible? Anjali didn't want to think any more as she turned around and buried her face in the stranger's chest, needing the hug fiercely. She wasn't even aware that her arms had gone around the man's waist.

26

arth really didn't know what made him do what he did. But her body language appeared to call out to him. He held the woman close, not saying anything as words seemed superfluous. He could feel her pain, deep within him. Her face was buried in his chest, her body heaving with sobs. He let her cry her heart out, his large hand rubbing her back, doing his best to soothe her. Tears would definitely act as catharsis. Seconds flowed into minutes as he held her in his arms, while her sobs grew less desperate.

Calm reigned within a few minutes as the woman's body grew still. He waited for her to fully recover before offering her his snowy white handkerchief as she raised her head from his chest. Her nose was red, her eyes swollen. Parth couldn't fail to be fascinated despite all that. She took the handkerchief without raising her eyes to his face. "Thank you," she whispered, her voice hoarse. She wiped her face and blew her nose into it before looking at him, embarrassed. "I'm sorry. Let me have this washed and returned to you." The smile didn't reach her tear-drenched brown eyes.

Parth nodded, looking at her silently. The author in him woke up with a vengeance and he could feel his writer's block crumbling. This lovely lady truly inspired him.

"I'm Parth, Parth Bhardwaj," said he, a mite hesitant, as he wondered if it was the best time to introduce himself. But then, he wanted to know her more.

"Anjali Mathur," came the soft reply, her voice still rough with emotion. "You'll have to excuse me!" Saying this, the woman in mauve walked away swiftly, leaving Parth staring after her. His arms hung at his sides, missing her warmth.

Parth stood on the balcony, his back against the wall, looking in the direction she had gone. Anjali appeared to be in her mid-thirties and was obviously married as she wore *sindoor* on her forehead at the hair parting. What could have happened to upset her so badly, that too in the middle of a party? He hoped that nothing was seriously amiss.

She had felt good in his arms, he thought as a soft smile lit his rugged features. Parth shook his head as he reined in his thoughts. He steered clear of married women. There was bound to be trouble that way.

Once it became obvious that Anjali Mathur wasn't coming back, Parth walked down to the lower level to rejoin the party he had left.

27

njali felt shaken as she rushed away from the balcony, away from the man called Parth. What was wrong with her? How could she allow a stranger to hold her so close to his person? A shudder ran through her body as she recalled the few minutes in his arms. She refused to admit to herself that she had felt cherished during those moments as she had never felt in her entire life. Colour ran up her cheeks as she felt guilty of forbidden pleasure.

Parth Bhardwaj was obviously new in the Vermas' circle. She'd never set eyes on him before now. In the few seconds that she had looked at him, Anjali had registered that he was tall and handsome, obviously in his forties. What had struck her most were the piercing silver eyes on his tanned face, as if they could look into her very soul.

Anjali reached the bathroom set aside for the guests and her thoughts came to a stop when she heard her name.

"Did you see the way Anjali's husband was holding that new chick? He's obviously lusting after a younger woman," laughed Deepa, her words slurred as if she had had a drink too many.

"Hey, that's his executive assistant Seema. They've been going around since ages. What's a guy to do if he can't find love in his wife's arms?" roared Rita with laughter.

Anjali blanched as she walked away, looking for another washroom to clean up the ravages of her crying bout. Finding an empty one, she set about repairing the damage to her make-up, straightening her back defiantly. She wasn't going to take this insult lying down. Two could play at a game.

She walked downstairs as if nothing had happened and was glad to catch the eye of Parth Bhardwaj. He was standing at the bar and had obviously been looking out for her. He raised his glass in a toast, his right eyebrow up in query as if to ask if she was alright. Anjali gave him a small nod, her lips refusing to smile.

She saw him walk forward, excusing himself to the people around him. Anjali caught her husband and his secretary in her peripheral but refused to turn her head to acknowledge them. Parth met her at the end of the staircase and asked, "Would you care to dance?"

Anjali went along with him, her back straight and proud. Her escort was handsome and obviously game to spending time with her. She planned to make the most of it. That she felt treasured by his single-minded attention was an added bonus.

What she hadn't expected was the frisson she felt along her nerves when Parth's right arm went around her bare waist while he held her right hand aloft in a typical dancing stance. Their fingers were entwined while their palms were pressed close. Would he feel the pulse beating hard there?

The music had slowed down and the lights were dimmed. She became oblivious to the couples dancing around them as she moved in rhythm, her eyes caught up in his silver gaze. Their eyes held a conversation even as their lips remained silent.

Anjali breathed deeply, doing her best to calm her fast beating heart. She couldn't help but notice the intelligence which shone on the face in front of her. Parth had a broad forehead with thick, dark eyebrows. His cheeks were hard with a fuzz of dark hair that gave him a rugged look. He had a prominent beak of a nose and a strong chin. Yes, she couldn't help noticing that as she abhorred a weak chin for sure. Oh, and there was this cleft which gave him a completely sexy look.

Anjali brought her gaze down to his shoulder level. What was wrong with her? Had she just thought that the man she was dancing with was sexy? Oh my God! She placed her forehead on his shoulder, unable to meet his eyes with the kind of thoughts which were racing through her mind.

But that just brought her closer to his body. She felt helpless when he lifted the hand he was holding and placed it on his shoulder even as both his arms went around her waist. She refused to acknowledge that their hearts beat together in synchrony.

It was a long time before she could sense the whispers building around them. Right now, she couldn't give a damn.

It was past one am when Parth insisted on escorting Anjali back to her building. Jayant was nowhere in sight. Neither was his arm candy.

28

arth stayed up all night, typing away on his laptop, his creative juices flowing. The outing had obviously done him good. He had enjoyed the evening at the Vermas, what with the excellent Scotch, delicious food and a gorgeous woman who had danced with him all night.

While he had found out from someone that businessman Jayant Mathur was her husband, he stayed clear of being introduced to the man. Watching Anjali's husband flirting with another woman made Parth angry as he realised that that must have been the reason for her tears. Good for her that she had not taken it lying down.

Her dark brown eyes had been swimming in tears when he met her for the first time. When he had held her then, it was a platonic hug, offering solace.

But that wasn't the case when they had danced together. Her body had fitted perfectly in his arms while he had felt a powerful attraction flowing between them. And how could he miss the banked passion in her eyes? Her rosy lips would tempt a saint, and that tiny mole above her upper lip was an open invitation to be touched. How he had managed to stop himself was a complete surprise to him. He had to keep reminding himself that she belonged to someone else. Okay, her husband was a cad, but that was no excuse.

But he wouldn't have missed meeting Anjali Mathur for anything. It had been a sheer stroke of luck and had triggered off the writer in him with a vengeance.

It was ten in the morning when he finished checking the two chapters he had typed out—the ones he had planned to write the earlier day. He got up and stretched as he yawned, a grin breaking through the morning stubble. Thank God he was back on track! Feeling too alert to go to sleep, Parth went for a shower as he decided to take a walk. Maybe he could enjoy a coffee at the Cafe Coffee Day outlet in the complex.

Action following thoughts, Parth got ready and left his penthouse after twenty minutes. Thoughts of Anjali dogged him all the way. How much ever he tried to convince himself that she belonged to someone else, he couldn't stop recalling the feel of her soft body held against his.

Now where had that come from? He had just offered solace to a woman in emotional distress. Okay, she was attractive, no doubt about that. But she was married, for heaven's sake. He was careful not to even make a pass at a married woman. No way!

Parth shut his mind to thoughts of Anjali as he took out his cell to call his agent. "Ram, you'll be glad to hear that I've finished writing till Chapter Nineteen.

There are just three more chapters to go before you can send it to the publisher."

Parth moved his iPhone a couple of inches away from his ear as his agent whooped with joy, smiling as he entered CCD. He chatted for a few more minutes before disconnecting the phone and ordered himself a large cup of hot mochaccino, looking forward to the blend of freshly brewed coffee and chocolate. He scanned an eye over the snacks on display, not too keen on any of them. Sitting down at a table, he opened the newspaper which he had brought along with him. Within seconds, Parth was lost to his surroundings.

Jayant woke up like a bear with a sore head. He had been fuming from last evening. How dare she? How dare Anjali insult him like this, dancing away with another man, and a stranger at that? Parth wasn't part of their friend circle. In fact, none of the guests seemed to know him. Anjali's scandalous behaviour had been the talk of the party. Their hostess Ruchika had obviously been disgusted with the way Anjali had made an exhibition of herself. What a shame! How could he hold up his head in society?

Jayant had left the party immediately after midnight, with Seema on his arm. He had planned to spend a few hours with her at the service apartment maintained by his company which also served as a guest house. Being high-end, it gave the businessman all the privacy he needed.

But on reaching there, he had been too disturbed to take up Seema's invitation to bed. He tossed back a couple of more pegs of whiskey with soda, angry and restless. Anjali had never behaved like this before. For all her shrewish tendencies, she always treated her husband with respect. What had come over her today?

He suddenly upped and left the apartment, not saying anything to Seema. He got back home at around two am, planning to tell Anjali off for her frivolous behaviour. He entered their bedroom to find the bed empty. Where the hell was she?

He called her cell on speed dial and heard its ring. Following the sound, Jayant reached the living room to see it lying on a side table. She was obviously home. Then where was she?

He looked for her in the dressing room adjoining the bedroom, but she wasn't there either. Searching the apartment, he finally reached the furthermost bedroom and found it locked from inside. What? How can that be?

Had she brought her lover home? Jayant blanched. He knocked a couple of times but there was no response. Would Anjali stoop so low? Not knowing quite how to deal with the situation, Jayant walked back to their bedroom. Coming to a quick decision, he changed out of his suit and into pyjamas. Taking a couple of pillows, he settled for the night on the living room sofa. He would catch the culprit red-handed, that's what he would do.

He spent a terrible night in discomfort, in a state of half sleep. No wonder he woke up with a splitting headache and a ferocious temper.

"Anjali!" Jayant yelled the moment he opened his eyes. He looked at the clock to see that it was past nine. Well, it was Saturday so that wasn't an issue. But where the hell was his errant wife? He thought he heard music and followed the sound to the other bedroom to find the door open. His jaw dropped when he found Anjali calmly hanging her clothes in the wardrobe there, singing along with the music which blared from a speaker.

"What the hell are you doing?" he asked, his voice menacing.

When no answer was forthcoming, he rushed over to her and putting a hand on her shoulder, turned her around roughly. "What the hell do you think you are doing?" he asked again, his face red with temper.

He blanched when his wife gave him a freezing look. He had never seen her like this before. Jayant's hand dropped as if burnt, his face shocked. He stood there in front of her, his throat clammed up at the indignant expression on her face.

njali had woken up from a restless sleep at 5.30 am. She stepped out of the guest bedroom to see her husband snoring away on the sofa. Though he didn't look very comfortable—and serve him right—he was still sleeping, unlike she who had tossed and turned the whole night.

It took her but an hour to move all her belongings to the corner bedroom. From now on, she decided that that would be her room. If Jayant didn't like it, he could sue her for all she cared. She wasn't going to put up with his insults and tantrums any more. Last evening had been the last straw.

It had been so against her nature to dance continuously in one man's arms, especially a stranger's. But just then Parth's silent support had been a balm to her frazzled nerves. Not once had he shown curiosity about her tears. He had not asked her one question. He hadn't even spoken much. He had kept her in a cocoon of warmth, safe from the others.

No, she wasn't going to think about Parth's charisma which had a strong pull on her senses. No way!

Given a chance, every one of the guests would have needled her over her husband's behaviour. But they had all stayed away, thanks to Parth.

And walking out of the party had not been an option. She had her pride too. Already people were gossiping behind her back, making her a laughing stock. If she had left, it would have made it worse. If her reputation had been in shreds by the time the evening ended, Anjali wasn't too bothered. What respect would she have in their eyes after the way Jayant had flaunted another woman in his arms? Anyway, Anjali didn't give a damn about those high society snooty coots. Not one could she call a friend.

And here she was, humming along with the music from the speakers attached to her phone, hanging her clothes in the wardrobe which had been rarely used. She felt freer than she had yesterday, as if she had finally taken the reins of her life in her own hands. She never heard Jayant call her.

She was startled when she felt her husband's hand on her shoulder as he turned her around roughly. Her adrenaline high, Anjali turned around to glare at him, her hand automatically pressing the stop button on her phone to shut down the music. Her dark brown eyes turned fiery with loathing as she looked at the man who had run her life from the day they were married. She had buried all her dreams and desires to adjust to his way of life, all the time subjugating to his will in every aspect. And this is how he repaid her loyalty. She owed him nothing.

She felt a moment of triumph when Jayant removed his hand from her shoulder of his own volition. That was a first indeed. She continued to look at him, waiting for him to say something.

"Where is he?" asked Jayant, his voice a snarl.

Anjali was amused more than anything when she saw the shock disappearing from his face to be replaced by anger. So! Her husband felt he had a right to be angry. His arrogance knew no bounds it seemed.

She raised an enquiring brow at him as she asked, "Who?"

"Your lover of yesterday of course, who else?" yelled Jayant in reply.

A sarcastic smile broke out on Anjali's face. "Please don't drag me down to your level Jayant. I'd never..."

"Don't lie. I know you brought that man home last night. I returned at two am to find this room locked from inside. Aren't you ashamed to behave like this in our home? Don't you have common decency...?"

Anjali raised a hand to stop the flow of words, her eyes spitting dislike. "You're a fine one to talk of decency. You left the party at midnight and reached home which is just a few buildings away only two hours later. Where did you disappear to in the meantime? Or should I not question you because you are the "man" of the house?" She raised both hands to make quotation marks in the air.

"What I do outside our home is none of your business," he said, his voice not so confident now.

"Thanks for the tip," said Anjali, her lips curling in disgust. She turned around to continue setting up her wardrobe.

31

Seema opened her eyes when she felt sunlight streaming through the glass windows. She could feel the heat of the rays despite the air-conditioner. It took her a couple of moments to realise where she was—on a huge empty bed in the service apartment owned by Jayant.

Her mouth drooped as a feeling of dejection swept over her. The first shock had hit her when she set eyes on Jayant's wife Anjali. It had been difficult holding herself together at the party after that. Seema had felt as if everyone was looking at her with a smirk on their face. She had been unable to bear the shame of it. Jayant had been loud and raucous as always, enjoying himself to the hilt. That his friends were ignoring Seema didn't seem to matter to him. She had just shrunk in shame. There had been no way out as Jayant had held her to his side, his arm around her, throughout the evening. She didn't fail to notice that his hold had become tighter from the moment his wife began dancing with another man.

Seema couldn't blame the woman. Shrew or not, no wife deserved her husband to treat her so shabbily.

She was shocked by her boss-turned-lover's behaviour. He had been unfair to both his wife and girlfriend, bringing them to the same gathering.

She had been relieved when they left the party at midnight, even though it was going full swing. Anjali hadn't stopped once as she continued to hog the dance floor. And she hadn't bothered to change partners. Was the woman having an affair with that fellow? Well, who was Seema to throw stones from her glass castle!

Seema was ready to forgive Jayant anything when he took her away from the party. But he had continued to drink, brooding as he sat on the sofa, his tie askew. She went to shower and change into a transparent negligee, hoping to create a mood more conducive to lovemaking. But he had simply stared at her, not really looking as he tossed a glass of whisky and soda back into his throat.

Her second shock had come when he walked out of the apartment, without uttering a word. What was wrong with him today? She had been sure till yesterday that Jayant would fall in love with her over time. But... did she really know him? Seema was extremely upset.

She had dragged herself to bed, feeling lonely and sorry for herself. It was too late to take a cab back to her tiny flat in Mulund. And anyway, her home was also empty. Might as well relax in the luxury of this place!

She had sent messages to Jayant on Whatsapp, but he hadn't bothered to reply. Seema couldn't remember when she fell asleep as she stared at her phone, willing it to ping.

She checked the phone on waking up to see that Jayant had still not replied, though he had obviously seen her messages. Was his interest in her waning? Insecurity ate into Seema as she changed into a pair of jeans and t-shirt which she had carried in her overnight case. Packing her discarded clothes of the night, she left the apartment, locking it behind her. The long weekend loomed in front of her, lonelier than ever.

ayant was flabbergasted by the turn his life had taken over the past week. From domestic bliss it had changed overnight into a war zone—a cold one. Anjali thwarted him at every turn, mutiny at its peak.

To begin with, she refused to return to their room, insisting on staying in her new bedroom. Music blared there during all waking hours, extending to the wee hours on most nights. His requests and even orders that she turned the volume down fell on deaf ears.

And the mornings! Though he had been aware that Anjali didn't really like setting out his clothes for the day, he hadn't been too bothered about it. After all, it was her duty as his wife to care for him. But these days, she didn't bother to wake up before he left for work. Jayant's blood pressure rose every day—more and more. But the wife who used to work hard at keeping him calm and happy seemed to have disappeared forever. Not that he had appreciated it over the past twenty years. But then, that was what wives were for, right? He couldn't understand what had come over her. That it could be his fault never even struck him.

She always informed him whenever she went out and of course she told him where she went. Over these past few days, all that had gone for a toss. It had been the last straw yesterday when he got back home at eight pm to find only the cook Sita there.

"*Memsaab kho bhulao,*" said Jayant, walking into his bedroom. He stepped out after fifteen minutes to find Sita standing near the sofa, wringing her hands. "What did I tell you?" he barked. Bloody servant! Couldn't follow one instruction correctly.

"*Saab,* madam *ghar par nahi hai,*" said Sita.

Jayant's anger knew no bounds. Where the hell was his wife? He did not want to ask the cook about Anjali's whereabouts. What would she think of him if she realised that he had no clue about his wife's comings and goings?

He dismissed her with a flick of his hand before pouring himself a glass of whiskey and soda. He brooded as he sat on the sofa, surfing channels on television, until he heard the key in the lock. Looking at the clock, he was shocked to see that it was way past eleven. What the hell!!

"Anjali, where have you been?" Jayant's voice was mild when he asked her that question. He didn't want to trigger off the ticking bomb which walked in the guise of his wife nowadays.

"I thought it didn't matter what I did outside our home," replied Anjali in a cool voice before walking towards her bedroom.

"Wait!" Jayant's voice went up by several notches. He saw her stop in her tracks though she didn't bother to turn towards him. He walked up to her and spoke softly once again. "Anjali, I really don't know why you are doing what you are doing. But it's high time you got back to normal. You've had your fun, being away from me. But come on, let's get our lives back on track. Let's have dinner." He raised his voice again to call, "Sita, serve the food."

"I've had dinner."

It took a few moments for it to register with Jayant that his wife had replied to him, mainly because those weren't the words he had expected to hear from her. His mouth fell open in astonishment as he watched on in silence while she continued on her way to her room.

That's when Jayant realised that he had completely lost control of his married life. Was there anything he could do to regain it?

S ita had been really tense about her boss's reaction to his wife's absence. He always knew where she was. The cook had never faced such a situation. Today, Anjali madam had left the house at around six pm.

"Sita, I won't be home for dinner. *Saab* will be, so make his favourite *Thai curry* and *steamed rice*," she had said before leaving.

Sita hadn't given any thought to the situation. The high society couple lived like that only. Who was she to judge them!

But what she hadn't expected was for Jayant to walk in late in the evening to ask for his wife. Didn't he know that she had gone out? Sita wasn't stressed about her mistress's safety, just how her boss would react. He had a bad temper.

What would he say if Sita told him that Anjali madam wasn't home? Well, she didn't have a choice but to tell him so. And when she did, Sita was relieved that he dismissed her without saying anything.

But even Sita was surprised when Anjali madam returned home after eleven o'clock. She knew as she had been waiting to serve dinner to her boss. She heard them talking for a few minutes before she heard Jayant sir calling out her name, telling her to serve the food.

Sita got up from the floor and opened the food warmer to remove the dishes, taking them to the dining table where a single place was already set. She could sense her boss fuming as he ate his dinner silently, without relishing it. A small frown puckered Sita's forehead as she watched him in silence from further away, waiting on him. She had never seen him so quiet. She was worried that he might blast any time soon.

Sita thanked her lucky stars when Jayant got up from the dining table without uttering a word. She hurriedly cleared the table before rushing to the safety of her tiny abode behind the kitchen.

34

arth was on a remote seashore in the arms of a beautiful lady, loving every inch of her. The sound of the waves played soothing background music as she responded to his touch like a finely tuned violin. Her brown eyes gazed at him adoringly, even as she ran her soft hands through his hair. Luckily, there was no one else on the beach as both of them were naked, entwined in each other's arms. Gentle waves touched their feet now and again as they made ardent love. Parth groaned as she pressed her lips to his neck, her sharp teeth nipping him as their passion built to a crescendo. Lovemaking had never been so good before!

Thoroughly satisfied, Parth was basking in the aftermath when he suddenly woke up to realise that he had been dreaming.

He blanched as he recognised the face in his dream. No! Not her! She was married. Okay, not happily, but that still didn't stop her from being Jayant Mathur's wife.

He had truly made all efforts to erase memories of Anjali as he continued to write his novel. However hard her face tried to superimpose over his laptop screen, Parth managed to push her away as he worked diligently. He was almost done and no woman was going to distract him from his purpose, especially not someone who was wedded to another man. There were no two ways about it.

What he had not expected was for Anjali to invade his dreams. While he could control his thoughts with iron determination, what the hell could he do when he was asleep? Parth shook his head vigorously as he got out of his bed, automatically folding his comforter and straightening the sheet. He gave the pillows a couple of vicious punches before placing them against the bed head. He will not think about her!!!

He switched on the electric percolator, adding a few spoons of filter coffee blend to it. Pouring water into the other side, he went to the bathroom to get ready for the day. The smell of coffee invaded his nostrils as Parth walked back into the kitchen, his hair damp from the shower. He wore a pair of denim shorts teamed with a white t-shirt. Pouring a cup of steaming hot coffee, he added some sugar and milk before walking to the balcony.

The view from the thirty-fifth floor never failed to thrill him. He stood there, watching fluffy white clouds sailing across an azure blue sky, sipping the fragrant coffee. The people on the ground failed to distract him as they appeared tiny from his vantage point. He breathed in deeply, stretching his arms luxuriously. What a beautiful day! He decided to work in the balcony today. Just one more chapter to finish! This was no time for distractions.

35

The past week had taken a toll on Anjali. Being peace loving, she had tolerated her husband's bossy behaviour all these years, keeping her thoughts and feelings buried deep within her. It had been easier to fall in with Jayant's wishes than to take a stand. The few times she had tried had always led to temper tantrums on his part. She had given up after a point and continued to live the life of a doormat.

But he had gone too far at the Vermas' party. Though deep within she was the same peace-loving and harmonious Anjali, the time had come to put her foot down. And she did it in the only way she knew how; by refusing to listen to Jayant, whatever he said.

Last night's outing had been in complete defiance. But the problem was that it had backfired on her. She hadn't gone all that far. Not having close friends, Anjali decided to roam the rose garden at Hiranandani Gardens. That had taken her a little more than an hour. She had left home early evening as she was keen to be out of the house before Jayant came home and she hadn't known when he would return.

With too much time on her hands, she went to Starbucks Coffee and hung out there for a couple of hours, nursing a cup of cold coffee with choco chips floating in it. Luckily, she had carried a book with her and it hadn't been too difficult. She had found a corner sofa which kept her out of sight of nosey neighbours. From there, she had taken off to Mia Cucina to have dinner. She was glad that her appetite had not deserted her as she tucked into a portion of *tagliatelle al pesto*—homemade pasta in creamy basil pesto sauce, washing it down with peach iced tea.

Finally, it was time to go home. Checking her wristwatch, Anjali was startled to see it was almost eleven. Mentally shrugging a shoulder, she got up to leave for home.

It hadn't been easy facing Jayant, walking into their flat so late at night, without having informed him prior to going out. She had never done this before and she didn't really enjoy it. Refusing to meet her husband's eyes, Anjali had walked away from him after refusing dinner and entered her room.

She had a quick shower and wore a nightie before settling on her bed. Sleep hadn't been easy coming as Anjali tossed and turned on the bed for a long time. Finally, she fell into a fitful slumber at around three in the morning.

Waking up just before noon, Anjali felt a bitter taste in her mouth. What had she achieved last evening? Her mind went around in circles. Okay, she had established that she will not be under Jayant's thumb. Fair enough! But how did that enhance her life? She was even now the same Anjali, living in his home, dependent on him financially. She had nothing to call her own. Okay, he had bought a few properties in her name. But so what? That still hadn't improved her humdrum existence one iota.

Should she get back to learning music? Or what? Somehow, the idea didn't appeal to her. The day stretched out in front of her, same as before, as Anjali's lips drooped in sadness. Was there a purpose to her existence?

That day, Anjali went down to CCD and was glad when she found it almost empty, before someone waved to her! It was none other than Parth Bhardwaj. Her face went pale in response as she walked in his direction. She didn't quite understand her reaction to the man, though one thought was foremost in her mind—he had seen her at her weakest, something no other human being had seen, ever. Another part of her mind insisted that he had been her strength that night, the one who had ensured that she hadn't fallen apart.

Throughout her life, it was only Arjun who empathised with Anjali. But then, his being her son and way younger than her, she had been careful not to rely on him too much.

Parth was in a different league. He was an adult male and he had offered her solace. Not happy with the unfamiliar feelings and sensations churning within her, she had shoved all her thoughts about him deep within the recesses of her mind and decided to forget him after he left her at the entrance to her building the other night.

Meeting him today was unexpected. *Or was it?* asked a soft voice from within. She was aware that he stayed in the same colony. Had she been walking around the area these past two days, inadvertently looking for him?

Parth had got up by now to take her hand in his, a smile on his face. "Anjali, we meet again." He pulled a chair for her, solicitous to the core, scoring another point in her eyes. "What shall I get you?"

"I would love to have a chocolate frappe. I'll ..."

"Relax, let me get it for you," said Parth before walking to the counter. Anjali watched on helplessly. It was a novel experience being waited on by a man.

She looked down at her hands which were pleating and un-pleating her *dupatta,* feeling apprehensive. At the party, Parth's presence had been a blessing in disguise. But she hadn't wanted to meet him again. He was a strange male and she was a married woman. That his strong and calm presence, emanating warmth, attracted her was something Anjali was petrified of admitting, even to herself.

She looked up nervously when he came back to sit in front of her, too close for comfort. Too close as she was only too aware of how it felt to be in the cocoon of his arms. Anjali blanched! Now where had that come from?

Neither of them said a word until a waiter brought their orders and placed the tray on their table.

"I thought we could share some *banana cake,*" said Parth as he pushed the tray closer to her. He added some Demerara sugar to his coffee, mixed it before lifting it to his lips, his piercing silver gaze never leaving her face.

"Not for me, thank you," said Anjali before lifting her glass of milkshake to take a small sip through the straw. She didn't think she would survive sharing anything with him. She refused to look into his all-seeing eyes.

Parth shrugged as he forked a piece of cake into his mouth. "So, how are you today?" he asked.

Anjali lifted heavy eyelids to look at him for a couple of seconds before bringing her gaze down to the table. "I'm good," she said in a whisper.

"Do you want to talk about it?" he asked, his voice gentle.

Her eyes turned damp with a sheen of tears when she heard the compassion in his voice. She shook her head, continuing to concentrate on her drink.

Parth drank his coffee in one go, waiting for her to finish hers. He got up immediately and said, "Let's go."

She didn't ask him 'where' as she followed him out of CCD. His building was barely a two-minute walk and they took the elevator up to his penthouse. Parth opened the door and led her in, switching on the air-conditioner. He sat her down on a sofa and took the one opposite hers. "Talk to me," he said, his voice compelling.

It all came gushing out as Anjali poured her heart to him. Tears flowed unchecked down her face as she spoke to him, her hand holding on to his tightly. Somehow, it was easy to talk to this stranger who was an excellent listener.

"I don't really know what's happening to our marriage. I was not even twenty when I married Jayant. He was building his business those days. I'd been brought up to believe that being a housewife was the most important thing in a woman's life." Anjali cleared her throat as it threatened to block her, before continuing, "Today I find myself at a loose end, not understanding the purpose of my life. Arjun, my son, is all grown up and has taken off to live his own life. Jayant is too busy with his business and other activities to have time for me. Not that I blame him. But what do I do? He and many of the people we know believe that I have the best possible life, with a lot of time and money on my hands and freedom to do what I please."

"Freedom!" Anjali laughed at herself bitterly. "I don't know the meaning of the word. I'm Jayant's chattel, always at his beck and call. I can't lift a finger without his permission. And he doesn't want me to be involved in any activity which doesn't revolve around him." She looked up at Parth with pathetic eyes. "Where am I going wrong? Is everyone else right? Am I being unreasonable wanting more out of life? Like Jayant is unable to understand why I am sick and bored of my existence. He feels I'm ungrateful, not appreciating what other women would give an arm and a leg to achieve. What's wrong with me Parth?"

Anjali was glad that he didn't interrupt her even once as she raged about the golden cage she lived in. And it was not long before Anjali found herself in his arms. She didn't know who made the first move, but there she was, feeling safe and comforted once again. She could feel his large hand on her back, patting her like one would a small baby. Her sobs reduced slowly to hiccups as she calmed down in his arms. She held on to him tightly, her arms around his waist. He didn't utter a word. He was just there, like a rock in the midst of a stormy ocean.

Soon, the pain in her shifted to a completely new feeling. Anjali became aware of the hard planes of his chest to which her body was pressed tightly, even as she breathed in the spicy cologne he was wearing. She realised that he had a perfect V-shaped body, his broad chest tapering into a narrow waist around which her arms clung. Her face was buried against his chest and she didn't want to leave his arms, ever. She felt his lips press to the top of her head and felt a tingle begin there to flow all the way through her body to the tips of her toes. A huge sigh shook her being when she felt his lips move to her forehead and then her cheek. While her mind nudged her to move away, her body refused to co-operate even as she felt Parth's warm breath in her ear as his lips moved to her throat, to touch the wild pulse beating there.

Anjali shuddered as her inherent sense of caution reminded her that they were all alone in his apartment. This wasn't right. She had no right to find comfort in another man's arms. If Jayant had extra-marital affairs, that was him. Anjali wasn't like that. She removed her arms from Parth's waist and pushed him away. She wasn't sure if she should feel relieved or upset when he let her go immediately. Walking a few feet away from him, Anjali rubbed a trembling hand over her face.

"Thank you, Parth," she said in a barely audible whisper, even as she picked up her handbag which had fallen on the floor beside the sofa. Not uttering another word, she walked away, determined to leave Parth's home and life forever.

But removing herself from his presence did not necessarily mean that she could wipe Parth from her mind. His chivalrous nature and the respect with which he treated her were completely novel to Anjali. She couldn't help but compare him with Jayant and find her husband wanting.

All of which was fine! That still didn't give her a right to feel attracted to another man. No way! Torn by the tug-of-war within herself, Anjali shut herself up at home, hating herself and her life.

36

Parth sighed as he watched Anjali leave his apartment in a rush. He wished, oh, how he wished that he only felt sorry for her. But he knew it was more than that. He was attracted to the woman and he felt terrible for her circumstances.

The outside world must be convinced that she led a pampered existence. But having a huge bank balance need not automatically mean a life of joy. Parth had an idea of what she must be undergoing as Jayant Mathur's wife—partly from what she said and the rest from what he gleaned from her body language.

He sighed again. Women were such complicated creatures and it wasn't easy to understand them. But every human being wants to be loved. Which was why Anjali was bereft—due to the lack of love in her life, and the want of a purpose. She had obviously lived her life vicariously through her son all these years. Now that he had left the nest, she was feeling lost.

Mathur was a typical Indian male it seemed. His wife served a purpose in his life and he obviously never considered that she was a living being with feelings of her own.

Parth had had his share of love affairs. But then, it couldn't be otherwise, his having reached the age of forty-two and having travelled around the globe. He had never felt the urge to settle down with a single woman. But even in an affair, he believed in being loyal to his partner. He couldn't relate to a man cheating on his wife. If Mathur had lost interest in his wife, it would be kinder to divorce her. It was obvious that the man was using her as it was convenient.

But then, it was all fine to pass judgement over someone. He wasn't living their lives for them. While Parth felt sad for Anjali, and was ready to offer his shoulder for comfort, he was also clear that her life was none of his business. At least it shouldn't be.

Okay, he was attracted to her was another matter. But then, he didn't plan to do anything about it. Maybe it was time he found a woman for himself, even if on a temporary basis. The last time he was in a relationship was more than a couple of years ago.

Parth firmly shut Anjali out of his mind and went back to work.

37

Jayant couldn't believe his eyes when they fell on Anjali three days later. It was not as if they hadn't been living on the same premises. But somehow, he never saw her around at home. Not that his life was affected in anyway. His meals were made available, his clothes in place. All messages which came for him were neatly written out on sticky notes and posted where he wouldn't miss them. He really had no cause for complaint. But he definitely didn't like it that his wife wasn't available at his beck and call.

Today, he decided to leave his office and go home immediately after lunch. He needed to talk to Anjali and find out when she planned to get back to normal. He never even imagined that she might not.

He rang the bell to have Sita open the door for him. He saw Anjali at the dining table and went to sit there beside her. He was shocked out of his wits when he looked at her face. It was wan and her hair was a mess, as if she had been running her fingers through it time and again. And she was shifting the *roti* and *sabzi* around in her plate, staring at it unseeingly.

"Anjali." he called softly.

Two lifeless eyes looked up at him. Where was the fire? The defiance? This woman wasn't the virago who had come home so late only the other night. Was that only five days ago? What had happened to her? Was she ill?

"What's wrong Anjali?" asked Jayant. "Are you unwell?" He placed the back of his hand on her forehead to check for fever. He was pleasantly surprised that she didn't move away from his touch. But his joy was short-lived when Anjali fell off the chair in a dead faint.

Jayant panicked. Anjali never fell sick. He shouted, "Sita, *jaldi aajao.*" When the cook came running, he told her to take care of her mistress as he dialled their family doctor.

"Narottam, this is Jayant, Jayant Mathur. There's an emergency. Please come home immediately. Anjali has fainted."

He disconnected the phone the moment Dr Narottam Pai agreed and turned to see Sita attending to his wife who was seated on the sofa.

He went to sit beside her and put his arm awkwardly around her shoulders. "Relax Anjali. Narottam should be here in a few minutes. Do you want to drink something? Sita, get madam some cold lemon juice with sugar and salt," he ordered.

The doctor arrived before Sita brought the juice.

38

r Narottam Pai had been General Physician to the Mathurs even before Jayant had married Anjali. Later, he was the one the young parents had rushed to, every time Arjun had the mildest of colds. Being from the older generation, the doctor had a reassuring demeanour. All his years of experience gave him the knowledge to treat his patients based on checking their pulse more than rushing for modern medical tests. All the three Mathurs had great faith in him.

He settled on the single sofa opposite Anjali as he checked her pulse. After examining her chest and back with his stethoscope, he looked at the dark circles under her eyes. "What happened to you Anjali? You haven't been eating your meals. *Kyun* Sita?" he turned his kind gaze towards the cook, "*tumhari madam barabar khana nahi kaathi hai kya?*"

"*Ji, Doctorji,*" replied Sita in a timid tone. Dr Pai saw her eyes moving towards Jayant and then Anjali before she turned to him, shaking her head, "*teen char din se madam khana barabar nahi kaa rahi hai.*"

Dr Pai raised a hand to stop Jayant from saying anything as he turned to Anjali again. "Are you upset about something Anjali? Worried about Arjun?" he asked gently.

The desultory glance Anjali gave him pained the doctor. She was obviously suffering from depression and that was probably the reason why she wasn't eating well. He had seen this problem time and again with rich men's idle wives. No one realised the importance of keeping a mind busy; idle minds being the devil's workshop and all that.

He wrote a prescription for some vitamins and handed it to Jayant. He spoke to Anjali again. "All the medicines in the world cannot cure you unless you have your meals regularly." He smiled at her and was disturbed when there was no answering smile from her. It looked like her condition was worse than what he had suspected.

He told Sita to give his mistress the lemon juice which had been kept on the side table. As the cook held the glass for Anjali to sip from, he gestured to Jayant to follow him and got up from the sofa.

He spoke softly so that only Jayant could hear what he had to say. "Listen Jayant, your wife is suffering from severe depression. She needs to see a psychiatrist immediately. Let me..."

"What? Are you suggesting that my wife has gone mad?" asked Jayant, a heavy frown on his face.

The doctor shook his head vigorously. "No Jayant, of course she's not mad. She's depressed. She needs treatment for that."

"Why can't you treat her for depression? Why does she need to go to a psychiatrist? You know how it is in our society, Narottam. People will talk. I'll never live it down. And imagine Anjali's life after visiting a psychiatrist. She'll be dubbed crazy," said Jayant, his voice insistent.

Dr Pai sighed. "If it was within my capacity, I would have definitely treated Anjali, Jayant. She's like a daughter to me. But you need to understand that her condition is severe. The sooner she sees a good psychiatrist, the better chances for her improvement." He took out another sheet of prescription and wrote down a name and phone number after checking his mobile. "Here, take this, Dr Nalini Singh is a professional and has more than twelve years of experience in this field. She will definitely be able to treat Anjali swiftly."

Jayant shook his head, taking the paper from the doctor, not even bothering to look at it. He placed it on the table near the door. The doctor left the flat after wishing him 'good luck'.

That night, the family physician called Arjun Mathur in England and explained the circumstances to him, insisting on the importance of his mother's treatment. It was beyond the call of a doctor's duty, but then, he was close to the Mathur family. And he was also aware of Jayant's dogmatic nature.

39

njali was very well aware that she was feeling low, and also the cause for it.

The past three days had been sheer torture, living with her thoughts which kept revolving around Parth. How could she pine for another man? Yes, she did pine for him and she had finally accepted it.

For the first time in her life she had felt pampered, wanted for herself, only when she was with Parth. She felt beautiful even as she felt the strong sense of attraction when she recalled Parth's lips on her face. She touched her forehead and cheek where he had kissed her, while she checked herself in the mirror, wondering if she looked different because of his kisses. All she could see was a woman who appeared wild, her hair unkempt, stark pain in her eyes.

Anjali felt torn, as never before in her life. The pain she felt now was a million times worse than what she had felt when she saw Jayant holding Seema in his arms the other evening. But that day, it was her ego which was hurt. Today, she felt crushed.

But why? How could she feel attracted to another man? She was married to Jayant and she needed to remain loyal to him, didn't she?

No wonder she had fallen sick. Only she didn't know how terribly depressed she was.

Arjun rang the bell to his home.

Dr Narottam Pai had sounded quite worried on the phone yesterday. It had been five in the evening when the call came. Arjun immediately packed a bag and left for the airport. He planned to catch the earliest flight home.

Why hadn't his father called him? His parents obviously thought they shouldn't worry him. He decided not to inform them of his imminent arrival in Mumbai. What if they told him not to come?

Once he had booked into a late-night flight to Mumbai, he called Jane to tell her about his plans.

"Oh Arjun! I hope your mom's alright. You go on, honey, and take care of her. I'm sure she'll be better the moment she sees you. And do give my love to your parents," said Jane.

Arjun talked for a while longer and finally disconnected the call after blowing her a kiss. He bought himself a sandwich and coffee at a restaurant before his flight was called.

And now, here he was the very next afternoon. He was surprised to see his father opening the door. He never did. Smiling at the startled expression on his father's face, Arjun walked into the house and hugged him.

"Hello Dad!"

"Hey Arjun! What are you doing here? Without a word too. Holidays were declared suddenly or what?"

"Just felt like meeting you and mom. Missed you guys. So, I took a couple of days off and caught a flight." Arjun didn't let on that Dr Pai had called him. "Where's Mom?" he asked, walking further into the hall. His dark brown eyes searched for his mother. This was the first time she hadn't rushed to meet him the moment he entered his house.

Arjun was surprised when his father took his hand and walked him to the furthest bedroom which usually served as a guest room. He went into the room with his father, a small scowl on his face.

His face paled when he saw his mother sitting on the bed, propped up by pillows. She was a frail shadow of her original self. "Mom!" Arjun's voice almost broke as he rushed to her, holding his arms out. He hugged her close, not failing to notice her desperate grip on his back when she returned his hug.

He held her for a while, waiting for her to calm down and then sat down to hold her face by the chin. "What's wrong, Mom?" he asked, feeling tearful. He had never seen his mother ill, ever.

"I don't know Arjun. I really don't know," she told him in a broken voice before leaning against the pillows once again. Her listlessness bothered him more than anything else.

He looked at his father, his right eyebrow raised in question and was surprised to see his father shrug in reply.

"I'm hungry. Is there anything to eat?" asked Arjun, hoping to distract his mother from her misery. He knew his mother couldn't see him go without food.

Anjali looked blankly at him. "Do you want to ask Sita?" she said, a frown of concentration on her face.

Arjun got up. "Why don't you come with me? I think you can do with some food too." He gently pulled at his mother's hand. The doctor had insisted that she was suffering from mental depression and that it was showing on her physical health.

"I'm not hungry Arjun. Why don't you go and eat?" Another first. No one could have stopped his mother from keeping him company whenever he had a meal at home.

"I don't want lunch if you don't come with me, Mom," said Arjun, his voice insistent.

Sita came into the room with a food tray for Anjali. She gave Arjun a relieved smile as she asked, "*Kaiso ho* Arjun *baba*?"

"*Mein theek hoon* Sita *mausi*," said Arjun, his replying smile not quite reaching his eyes. "Thank you for bringing our lunch here. Mom and I will eat together. Have you had yours Dad?" he asked his father. At his father's nod, he turned towards his mother, placing the tray on a small table which Sita set up in front of Anjali on the bed.

He didn't miss Anjali's disgusted look at the tray. It really got him worried. Could depression do this to a person? Or was it something worse than what Dr Pai believed?

He decided to tackle the matter after feeding his mother. It was a long drawn out process, but Arjun ensured that she ate every single morsel which was served on her plate. He ignored his mother's angry protests as he fed her like a small child.

Sita handed over the two pills which Anjali was to take after lunch. Arjun persuaded her to swallow those too. "Do you want to sit at the dining table with me Mom? I'm going to have lunch."

"No Arjun, I'm too sleepy," said Anjali, before turning around and sliding into a restless sleep.

A highly worried Arjun pulled the comforter over her and left the room, closing the door silently behind him.

His father was waiting for him at the dining table, where a single place was set for Arjun.

"What's happening Dad? What's wrong with Mom?" he asked, his voice breaking. Arjun cried on his father's shoulder, as the older man held him, patting his back awkwardly.

41

njali tossed and turned on her bed. Deep down she felt a strong urge to get up and spend time with her son. But her body refused to cooperate. The sleeping pill didn't help either. She was in a state of limbo—half-awake and half-asleep.

But she needed to get out of this. It made no sense feeling sorry for herself. She had so much to be thankful for. Look at her son Arjun. He had grown into a strapping young man and so loving too. What if her husband didn't care for her? It wasn't the end of the world.

It had been a mistake not attending her yoga and meditation sessions. But then, she had lost the will to go on over the past few weeks.

It was one thing to know that her husband flaunted his mistresses in front of their neighbours and friends. It was another to know that she had also committed the sin of feeling attracted to another man. If what Jayant did was wrong, then she wasn't right either. So, she hadn't had a physical relationship with the man. But she was captivated by Parth, powerfully. Given a chance, Anjali was scared that she might have an affair with the guy. Where was the sanctity of marriage?

Anjali turned back one more time, her bedspread bunching beneath her. That's when she noticed Arjun seated on a chair next to her bed. He was leaning back, fast asleep, his mouth slightly open. He was bound to have a crick in his neck when he woke up.

"Arjun?" Anjali put a hand on his knee and shook it. Feeling weak, her touch was feather light. But Arjun woke up immediately, rubbing his eyes and smiling at her.

"Mom, you are awake."

"Yes, Arjun. Why are you sleeping on the chair? You'll hurt yourself." Her voice was stronger than before.

"Not as much as you seem to be hurting Mom. Why are you so sick?" he asked, worry in his voice.

A tear slid down Anjali's cheek as she sniffed.

"I'm okay Arjun. There's nothing wrong with me."

"Really? Look at yourself Mom. Have you seen yourself in the mirror recently? You aren't the mother I left behind. Do you want me to return home? I can..."

Anjali looked at her son in shock. "Are you crazy Arjun? It's your dream to study at Kingston University. It's been barely six months and you want to quit? What's the matter with you?" Her voice grew stronger.

"There's nothing the matter with me Mom. Do you think I can study abroad at peace if you are suffering from poor health?" asked her son.

"This is a passing phase Arjun. I should be fine in a couple of days."

"That's awesome then. I'll leave the moment you are fine."

Anjali looked at him, a sigh escaping her, without her meaning to. Would she become alright in two days? She somehow doubted it. Her allure for Parth loomed in front of her mind's eye, condemning her.

42

Though Jayant didn't understand the concept of love, he was attached to his wife in his own way. He was extremely disturbed about her ill-health. But the seriousness of it hit him hard with the arrival of their son Arjun.

He got to know a day later that Arjun had come at Dr Narottam Pai's behest.

"But Arjun, Dr Pai has become old and is probably senile. He says that I should take your mom to a psychiatrist. He also insists that she's not mad. Then why would she need a shrink? I think it's best if we take her to Hiranandani Hospital and get her checked from top to toe. I'm sure they will diagnose her illness faster and will give her the correct treatment."

"Dad, what you are saying isn't a bad idea. But Narottam Uncle has been treating us all like forever. He knows us very well. He's an experienced doctor too. What's wrong in listening to his advice? He has even given you a reference," said Arjun.

Jayant was totally irritated. He didn't like the idea that his wife might be mentally unstable and wanted to keep his head buried deep in the soil. Dr Pai must surely be wrong.

"Arjun, you spoke to your mother. Do you think she's off her rocker?" he asked.

"Of course not, Dad. She's as sane as she can be. But," he insisted when Jayant opened his mouth to speak again, "she's terribly depressed Dad. I think it's the lack of a purpose or motivation. She doesn't have anything to look forward to; no reason to be up and about every morning."

It was obvious to Jayant that his son was terribly upset. But what the hell!

"What do you mean that your mom lacks motivation? She can do any damn thing she wants. She can go shopping whenever she pleases. She can have all the best clothes, jewellery or whatever she wants in the world. Do you know how many women would kill to be in her place?" asked Jayant, his voice rising as his temper surfaced.

"Dad!" Arjun's voice became softer in contrast. "What you're saying is all true. You have given her the best. But how much of shopping can one do, day after day after day? That's obviously not enough for Mom. She needs an occupation, some kind of an interest..."

"What nonsense are you talking Arjun?" Jayant didn't like the idea of his wife's attention deviating from him. "She has a full-time occupation of taking care of me. What more could she want?"

Arjun stared at his father, shaking his head slowly. "Let's do something Dad. Let's take Mom to Dr Nalini Singh, just one session. Let's see what the doc has to say about her. Better yet, why don't we ask Dr Singh if she'll visit Mom at home?"

Jayant thought about his son's suggestion for a minute before nodding his head. There was no reason to say 'no' to that. "Let's do it."

43

Though Dr Nalini Singh preferred to offer her consultancy in the front room of her ground floor apartment which had been set aside as a clinic, she did sometimes visit patients in their homes. And Anjali Mathur had been recommended by Dr Narottam Pai, one of her professors at college. She could never say 'no' to him.

It had been four days since Dr Pai had spoken to her about Mrs Mathur. And Dr Nalini Singh finally got a call from the patient's son, requesting her to go over to their home. Since she also lived and practised in Hiranandani Gardens, she just walked over to their building.

She stepped into the tastily furnished apartment of the Mathurs when Arjun opened the door. She sat with him for twenty minutes, asking a lot of questions about his mother—how she used to be and what she had become. The young man answered all her questions, while he looked anxious, his brown eyes troubled.

Nalini smiled at him as she said softly, "Don't worry, we'll get your mother up and about in the next few days. I will need to spend a couple of hours with her, without interruption."

A relieved answering smile lit his features as he replied, "Thank you, Dr Singh. That shouldn't be a problem. You go ahead with your examination. I'll be right outside and ensure that no one bothers you."

He guided Nalini to his mother's room. One look at Anjali Mathur and Nalini knew that the lady was severely depressed. "Hello, Anjali, I am Nalini Singh. I'm so glad to meet you. You have a gorgeous son here," she greeted, smiling gently at her new patient.

Nalini noticed that there was no answering smile on Anjali's face as she looked at the newcomer up and down. Sitting on the comfortable chair next to the bed, the doctor continued, "I live only a few buildings away, at *Athena*, on the ground floor. Isn't it surprising that we've never met?"

Nalini kept speaking softly, talking about herself, her hobbies, her pet cat and things along those lines. After about fifteen minutes, she was happy to see a glimmer of a smile on her patient's face.

The next two hours, Nalini drew out Anjali, gently but firmly; making her talk about her life, her day-to-day activities, her interests, her dislikes and more.

"I so enjoyed chatting with you Anjali. I would like to meet you again. Do you want to come over to my home? I have a cat. I am sure Simba will be thrilled to meet you," said Nalini.

Anjali nodded her head slowly. "I'd like that. Shall I come tomorrow?" she asked.

Nalini felt triumphant as she replied, "Sure thing. Do you want to take my cell number? Give me a call when you have a few minutes. We'll fix up and you come over."

She was glad to see Anjali get up from her bed, take her cell phone and feed in the number Nalini gave her. "Will you give me a missed call so that I can save your number too?"

Anjali nodded again before calling Nalini's cell. The doctor saved the other woman's cell number before getting up to take her leave. She went to Anjali and gave her a hug. "See you tomorrow."

44

rjun was happier now after meeting Dr Nalini Singh. The psychiatrist sure knew what she was doing. She had stepped out of his mother's room and said, "Arjun, you go and talk to your mother for some time. I am going back to my clinic now as I have another person coming in. We'll meet later today. There's no cause for worry. I will give you some medicines and also instruct you regarding her treatment. Who all are there in the family?"

"There's Mom, Dad and me. Yeah, then there's Sita *mausi*, the cook," replied Arjun.

"Okay! Will it be possible for you to come over to my clinic along with your father? Today itself if you can."

"Of course, Dr Singh. Shall I give you a call once I find out when Dad can get away from work? Your consulting hours are till nine pm, right?"

"Yes, that's right. See you later in the evening." Saying this, Dr Nalini Singh took her leave.

Arjun rushed over to meet his mother. He was surprised to see her sitting at the window, looking out. "Hi Mom!" he called out to her.

"Arjun!" Anjali smiled at her son for the first time since he returned home. "I like that lady, Nalini Singh. She's a good friend, unlike all the gossipmongers I meet at those parties. You know what? I'm going to her place tomorrow to meet her again. And she has a cat too. She says he will be thrilled to meet me. Isn't that nice?"

Arjun ran a hand over his eyes to wipe the tears which sprang forth. He didn't want to cry in front of his mother, especially now that she was looking so happy. "That's lovely Mom. And yeah, I liked that lady too. I am so glad you have a new friend."

He walked over and hugged her. She had lost quite a bit of weight and still looked weak. But he was glad to see that her smile was back in place.

"Hey, do you want to go for a ride?" he asked her.

Anjali shook her head. "Not today, Arjun. I still feel strange, as if I'm walking on air. Though I'm glad I could get up from my bed and sit at the window."

Arjun nodded to her, all smiles. "Then let's both listen to some thumping music."

Anjali giggled, obviously impressed by the idea. "Just hold my hand, will you? I will get back into bed."

Though Arjun didn't care for the idea, he didn't protest as he held his mother's hand when she walked slowly back to her bed. She was definitely better than what she had been when he came home.

She was asleep when Arjun and Jayant left to go to the doctor after eight pm.

45

Jayant was disgusted with the turn of events. For the first time he felt he was losing control of his life. He understood that people took ill with cold, fever, heart attack, high blood pressure or diabetes. And there were people who went mad and needed a shrink to treat them. He was aware of that too.

But what is this new thing called 'depression'? And there was a specialist to treat it too. He went along with his son to meet Dr Nalini Singh, though he didn't care for the idea. So, the doctor had met Anjali. She should just prescribe medicines, right? Why did she want to meet the rest of the family? Was this a new way of fleecing money? The cynical businessman couldn't see the point.

They didn't have to wait as the doctor's assistant immediately showed them into her clinic. Well, it looked more like a living room than a consultation; with comfortable sofas and even a couch. Jayant was convinced now that the doctor was after his money. He concluded that Dr Singh's flamboyant lifestyle must need a constant flow of cash to be maintained.

He sat next to Arjun on a double sofa while the doctor sat facing them. "Hello Mr Mathur! I met your wife today. She's simply delightful, a charming lady indeed."

Jayant nodded curtly, gritting his teeth. She seemed less and less like a doctor to him.

"Mrs Mathur is suffering from *Clinical Depression*. She…"

"But…" Jayant felt his son's hand on his arm when he interrupted the doctor. He saw the appeal in Arjun's eyes, requesting him to listen to the doctor fully. "Go on," he said.

"She has lost her appetite for food and her sleeping pattern has gone awry. She's been lucky in that she's been doing yoga and meditation regularly. That has ensured that she's not too far gone. I will prescribe her an anti-depressant. I have invited her over tomorrow, as a friend. For now, it's best she doesn't know that I am a psychiatrist treating her. What I need from you Mr Mathur, is a list of activities that the two of you do together—on a daily, weekly, monthly, and yearly basis. I'll need to study the pattern and will probably suggest a few changes which might help her in the long run."

Jayant glared at the doctor. What the hell! Why was she poking her nose into things which were none of her business? What he did with his wife was between the two of them. Why should he tell her anything? She was supposed to be treating Anjali. Look at her now, sitting there like royalty and questioning him as if he were in a witness box.

He put his thoughts into words, a frown on his face. "I don't understand. You are supposed to be treating Anjali, right? Why are you questioning me?"

Dr Singh replied softly, "I'm only trying to help your wife, Mr Mathur. You will need to co-operate. Treating her is not too difficult. She will come out of this with medication. But the more important thing is to ensure that she has no relapse. If that happens, there's no guarantee that she'll ever recover. The pattern will keep repeating. It's best you understand the repercussions. People who undergo clinical depression have a tendency to become suicidal. Mrs Mathur will need her family's support to come out of this totally. Since your son lives abroad, it's up to you to help her, Mr Mathur."

"I can take a break for six months, skip this semester and take the next one. Do tell me what needs to be done Dr Singh," said Arjun, much to Jayant's annoyance.

"Do you really think that's going to make your mother happy Arjun?" asked Nalini Singh. "And that should be the priority now. She needs to be kept cheerful at all times."

Jayant looked at the disappointment on his son's face and thought it best to play along. He didn't want Arjun to spoil his life, wasting the next six months, holding his mother's hand.

"Okay, tell me what you want to know, Doc. Let's get this show on the road."

It took Jayant less than five minutes to give the doctor a list of activities he did along with his wife. It equalled to zilch.

46

rjun shut his eyes in pain as he heard his father talk to Dr Singh.

Dinner at home together once in about ten days, lots of business parties every month—only there was not a single moment of privacy between the couple during those, and... that was it. Jayant had nothing else to say.

Arjun was truly shocked. They never went to movies, theatre or music shows together. He couldn't recall a holiday they had been on together—just the two of them. They had taken weekends off with other people always milling around.

While he was aware that his parents didn't have the best of relationships, that his mother was unhappy and bored with her life, he never knew they had no life at all together. Was that why she was sleeping in the other bedroom? That was the first thing which had struck him on the day he arrived, but how could he ask? This was one of the times when Arjun ardently wished he had a sibling to share his anxieties with. Being an only child was no fun at all.

Was it any wonder his mother was so ill? And he couldn't totally blame his father. It was a terrible twist of circumstances. All he hoped was that Dr Singh would be able to bring his mother out of it, back to the cheerful person she used to be.

"Dad, I think both of you need to go on a holiday, just the two of you. Go abroad, maybe Europe."

"Arjun, I can't spare that kind of time now, not when I am signing a new contract with someone," refused Jayant.

"But Dad, I don't mean immediately. Let's plan a trip a month or two from now. Mom also needs time to recover from her bout of sickness. Please Dad!"

"Let me see what I can do," said Jayant.

"You've to promise me Dad. Mom needs a change of scene. Greece will be a lovely place to go to. She..."

"But Arjun, your Mom will not go and relax there. She will want to run from one end of the country to the other. She's not even interested in shopping. She will want to see all those historical monuments and listen to the guides for hours together. She goes gaga whether it's a zoo or a museum. I can understand if she wants to relax in a gorgeous five-star hotel with a drink or two, exploring the local cuisine. But not your Mom," sighed Jayant, highly perturbed.

Arjun was visibly upset. His parents were too different from each other. He could see his father's point of view. He worked hard—sometimes 14-15 hours a day. His kind of holiday would be to go and chill somewhere. And his mother who was shut at home for most of her waking hours—with books and TV—would be keen to explore a new town.

How had the two managed to live as a couple for two decades? He was amazed!

47

njali looked forward to her outing to Nalini's home. She woke up the next day, feeling stronger than the past few days, her mind fresh. She wasn't aware that her medication had been changed last night.

She had a quick shower and dressed in a *salwar kameez* of brilliant orange and pink which reflected her sunny mood. She was on her way out when Arjun opened the door to her room.

"Mom," smiled Arjun.

"Hi Arjun, good morning! You're up. *Chalo chalo*, get ready fast. Let's have breakfast together. I need to go meet my new friend and her cat immediately after," she greeted her son in an excited voice.

"You want to go to her place after breakfast? Do you have her number, Mom? Why don't you give her a call and ask her if she's free? I'll get ready in the meanwhile."

"Oh yeah! That makes sense. We forgot to fix a time for my visit yesterday." She went back into her room to get her cell and dialled Nalini on her way out. She didn't notice her husband staring at her, looking irritated.

"Hello Nalini! Good morning," greeted Anjali enthusiastically. "When would be a convenient time for me to visit your home? I forgot to ask you yesterday. I can't wait to see you again and meet your little Simba."

"Do you want to come now? I'm free. You can have breakfast here with me," said Nalini, equally warm.

"Er... do you mind if I come over after breakfast? My son is here on leave. I'd like to spend some time with him. But of course, I'm keen to visit you after that. I'm sure he will want to meet his friends too."

"That's fine then. Shall I expect you in about an hour or so?"

"Perfect, Nalini. See you in an hour," replied Anjali, thrilled that she had a genuine friend to meet.

"I suppose you have completely recovered from whatever was ailing you," said Jayant, as he looked at his wife up and down.

"I think so too. I don't feel weak today. And my appetite's back with a vengeance," laughed Anjali, her cold war forgotten for the time being.

She walked to the kitchen to find out what Sita was cooking. "*Aloo paratha* with *pudina chutney* and *dahi kachumber*? Woohoo!" declared Anjali much to the cook's surprise. "Yes Sita, I'm very hungry today. Thank you for making my favourite meal," she said, hugging the other woman, bringing tears to her eyes.

"You sit down, *baabhi*. I will serve them hot," declared Sita, walking her mistress to the dining table.

Anjali sat down at the table to be joined by her husband and son. The three of them had a hearty breakfast as she talked and joked, obviously thrilled to have her son home and her health back.

"I'm leaving for Nalini's home after we are done here," she announced.

"Let me go with you, Mom. I'll leave you there and take myself off for a few hours until you are ready to return home." He got up to give her the morning dose of medicines.

"What are these for Arjun? Can't you see I'm perfectly alright?" said Anjali, her smile leaving her face.

"Aww Mom! You're feeling fine mainly because of the medication you had last night. The doctor changed your prescription. You'll need to complete the course, just over the next few weeks."

Anjali couldn't refuse her son, especially as he sounded exactly like her when she used to encourage him to have his medicines whenever he fell ill. She lifted a glass of water and swallowed all the three pills at one go and got up to leave. "Shall we?"

Jayant was non-existent for all the attention she gave him.

P arth walked into CCD in a jubilant state of mind. He deserved to celebrate and that meant he was ready to mingle with the public. His book was complete and had already been mailed to his agent.

He placed the order for his coffee and muffin and turned around to see a young man sitting alone at a table. The youth was busy typing with both his thumbs into his smart phone. Parth didn't know many people of that generation but this boy appeared familiar. Who was he? He never forgot people!

Walking over to him, Parth said, "Hey, do you mind if I sit here?"

The youth looked up at him with glowing brown eyes which were too familiar, though Parth couldn't place them. "Of course not, sir. Please do," he replied politely, pausing in his texting.

Parth smiled at him, a puzzled look on his face. "Thanks buddy. I'm Parth Bhardwaj. Have we met before?" he asked as he shook hands with the lad.

"I'm Arjun Mathur. And I don't think so," replied the boy with an answering smile on his face, also looking baffled.

Parth beamed in reply. "No wonder! You must be Anjali's son," he declared, confident that he was right.

Arjun's smile became wider. "You know my mom!"

"We've met a couple of times. And she does leave a lasting impression," said Parth, sipping his coffee.

"That must have been recent I suppose," said Arjun, obviously thinking. "Mom has never mentioned you."

Parth's eyebrows went up in query. "She talks to you? I'm sure she's missing you badly. By the way, how come you are here? I thought you study abroad, isn't it at Kingston University?" he asked. Once he was after answers, nothing stopped Parth from asking questions. It never struck him that he might be stepping past boundaries. As an author, he was sensitive. Then again, he loved to talk, get to know people, find out what made them tick.

Arjun looked amazed. "You must be a good friend of Mom's. When did you meet her last?"

"A couple of weeks back. Actually, right here at CCD."

Arjun sighed. "She's fallen ill. That's why I'm home."

Parth was shocked to put it mildly. Anjali was ill. His mind raced as he recalled their last meeting. She had been so upset with her life. But if her son was down in Mumbai because of that, what the hell was he doing here in the coffee shop instead of being at her side?

He frowned at Arjun. "Where is she? What's wrong with Anjali?"

Parth saw Arjun hesitate. "I hope you don't mind my asking questions Arjun. Your mother has become a good friend over the few times we met. You understand that I am worried," he said, a persuasive note in his voice.

Arjun spoke softly in reply. "She's suffering from Clinical Depression and is visiting Dr Nalini Singh at *Athena*. I'm waiting for her call to take her back home once they are done."

Parth saw the anxiety in the younger man's face as he himself turned pale. He instinctively held Arjun's hand in comfort. "You don't worry, son. Your mother's a fighter to the core. She will recover, sooner than you think."

He could see Arjun valiantly holding back his tears as he bent his head. "I don't know sir. I really don't know." He looked defeated.

Parth pulled his chair closer to Arjun's. "Call me Parth. Do you want to talk about it?"

rjun really didn't know what came over him. It wasn't in his nature to bare his heart to a stranger. But he was too upset about the weakening relationship between his parents, his mother's unexpected illness, and didn't know which way to turn. And Parth's eyes were so gentle and sympathetic. He poured his heart out to him. If he was his mother's friend as he claimed to be, then he automatically was Arjun's too.

If Anjali had been her normal self, she would have definitely told him about meeting Parth. Arjun was confident about that. That was the kind of relationship the mother and son shared.

"Mom is bored," he declared, as Parth nodded his head sagely. "She's not the type to sit around twiddling her thumbs. She's brainy and needs an occupation; something which will make her feel good. Dad doesn't understand. He thinks taking care of his needs should be enough. That probably used to hold good a couple of generations back. but not anymore. Mom has always listened to him, never crossed his wishes. But now it's telling on her mental health. She's unable to cope with boredom. I wish, how I wish..." his voice broke as he hid his face in his hands.

When Parth hugged him, Arjun turned to him for comfort, unknowingly behaving exactly like his mother, endearing him all the more to Parth.

Arjun felt himself drawn to the older man. He was a damned good listener. He moved away, a trifle embarrassed, and said, "Sorry about that, Parth."

"Not at all, buddy. What are friends for?" smiled Parth.

"Thank you so much for being here just now and listening to me, Parth. What do you do?" he asked curiously.

"I'm a writer. I write thrillers and travelogues. I live in *Olympus* on the thirty-fifth floor. You are welcome to my place at any time."

"Writer!" Arjun exclaimed in wonder. "Does Mom know that? We both love to read. Do you write by the name of Parth Bhardwaj?" he asked, unable to recall any author by that name.

Parth grinned, his white teeth shining brightly, shaking his head. "I go by a pseudonym. I write in the name of Paul Bainsbridge."

Arjun's jaw dropped, literally. He jumped up from his chair. "You are *the* Paul Bainsbridge?" he asked, his eyes rounded in surprise.

Parth nodded, obviously pleased. "You've read my books," he said, colour running up his tanned cheeks.

"Read? I know them by heart. You haven't told Mom obviously. She'll be thrilled to bits. She's a bigger fan than I am," he said, hugging Parth. He couldn't believe that he was chatting up the internationally famous author. "I can't believe this. And here I am, talking to you about my family problems. I hope I haven't bored you to death," said Arjun, feeling apologetic.

"If that's your reaction, I wish I hadn't given you my pen name, Arjun. I would rather be Parth to you and your mother." Parth was sincere.

Arjun looked into the author's eyes and read the genuineness there. "Thank you Parth, I'm honoured."

"About your Mom," Parth got back to the subject at hand. "She needs to get out of the house more. Have you thought of sending her on a holiday? To some faraway land? Travelling is good for the soul. I know from my experience."

Arjun was exuberant in his reply, "I'm glad you suggested travelling. That's what I told Dad. That he should take her abroad, maybe to Greece. I don't want her to go alone. She's spending too much time by herself as it is. And neither of them is keen that I drop this semester. Dr Nalini Singh is also against the idea. She's says that will make Mom sadder." His lips drooped as he finished talking.

"Hmm... the doctor's right and so are you. She shouldn't go alone. So, what does your father say?"

Arjun shook his head negatively. "Dad hates sightseeing. His concept of a holiday is very different from Mom's. I really don't know how they survived the last twenty years together." There, it was out, the main cause of his worry.

"Your mother could also find something interesting to do, on a day-to-day basis. She might not be keen to take a full-time job, but an occupation which keeps her busy for a couple of hours every day, will go a long way in healing her. What do you think?"

Arjun grinned at Parth. "I think it's an excellent idea. You mean some kind of freelance activity? Let me think. Well, she reads a lot, she knows how to browse the internet, she..." he stopped when Parth snapped his fingers.

"It's an idea. Do you think your mother will be interested in doing some research work for me? I'm planning my next novel and need to gather a lot of material on the subject. She just needs to compile a list of things which I require; save matter on a Word doc and maybe some links too. What say?"

"You're brilliant, Parth. That'll simply be amazing. Are you sure? Please don't do this unless you really need someone." He couldn't control the expression of hope in his eyes.

"Not at all, Arjun. Actually, your mother will be doing me a favour. I do hire someone on and off to do the research when I don't have the time to do it myself."

Arjun raised his hand in a high-five which Parth returned with equal fervour. "May I ask you another favour, please?" He continued when Parth nodded, "I'm not sure what Dad's going to say about this. I have an idea how to deal with him. Will you help me? I know it has nothing to do with you, but..."

"Don't be so formal, Arjun. Of course, it has a lot to do with me. Your mother's a friend. And so are you now. I want to help all I can. And the truth is that I need a researcher. It's a perfect package."

Arjun nodded vigorously, feeling lighter for the first time since Dr Pai's phone call.

50

r Nalini let Anjali into her consulting room with a smile on her face. "Welcome Anjali. I can see that you're absolutely fine today." She gave her a hug.

Anjali hugged her back with enthusiasm. "Yes, I'm much better. Thank you for inviting me to your place."

Nalini Singh refused to feel guilty for inviting Anjali over under false pretences. It was obvious that Anjali needed a friend—someone whom she could trust—more than a psychiatrist. If the only way to get her to respond was to lie, then Nalini would do it again.

She was passionate about her profession. Her main aim was to bring peace and joy to as many people as she could. She had achieved a lot during her twelve years of practice. There were many grateful patients who continued to remain her friends after recovering from their illness.

"Make yourself comfortable, Anjali. Do you want to lie down, maybe?" she gestured to the couch.

Anjali shook her head, her eyes taking in the bright and sunny room. "I'm fine. I can sit. You have a beautiful home, Nalini," she said.

Nalini smiled. "Thank you. Let's have some coffee together. Then I'll show you around. Unless you prefer tea?" She looked at her guest enquiringly.

"Coffee's fine," said Anjali.

Nalini rang a bell and a servant appeared. "Get two coffees please," said Nalini before settling down on a roomy single sofa opposite Anjali.

Just then, a black and white tom cat walked into the room. Nalini bent down to rub his velvety head before introducing, "This is my Simba. He's four years old and has been with me since he was a tiny kitten."

Anjali was down on her knees on the carpet, putting her hand out to Simba to smell, rapt attention on her face. Nalini was satisfied that her morning's work was already done as she watched her pet sniffing the new guest.

Anjali spoke to Simba as if he was a small child and the cat responded adoringly, rubbing his head against her legs. "When a cat rubs against your legs, it means he's accepted you," said Nalini, nodding to her maid to leave the coffee tray on a side table.

She poured the coffee into two cups and asked, "Do you take sugar, Anjali?"

Anjali got up from her crouched position on the carpet, her face glowing with joy. "Yes, I do," she said, accepting a cup.

They sat back sipping the coffee while Simba settled on the couch, licking himself.

"Are you a housewife too, Nalini?" she asked.

"I'm not married, Anjali."

"Oh!"

Nalini smiled when she saw Anjali's eyes go round in surprise. "I have been so caught up in my profession that I somehow never got around to finding a life partner." She hadn't regretted it so far.

"What do you do?" asked her guest.

"I'm a doctor," said Nalini, crossing her fingers surreptitiously. She didn't want to lose Anjali's trust.

"Oh, that must be the reason Arjun invited you home. I have been ill recently. Narottam Pai is our family doctor. He has been treating me these past few days; though for probably the first time, his medication didn't bring relief." Anjali grimaced.

"You're right, Anjali. Arjun invited me to your home because Dr Pai told him to. I..."

"I'm glad, Nalini. I'm truly glad I met you. I suppose it was you who gave me a change of prescription? I've never had a friend. Will you continue to see me after my treatment is over?" Anjali's eyes begged her.

"But of course, Anjali. Treating people is part of my profession. But I genuinely like you and would love to continue being your friend," smiled Nalini, relieved that she could be truthful now. She hadn't been sure how Anjali would receive the suggestion of meeting a psychiatrist. Her husband definitely hadn't cared for the idea; and Dr Pai had warned her of opposition.

Anjali got up and hugged her new friend, appearing emotional. Nalini hugged her back before they settled down to another long chat. Time flew on wings and it was already lunch time.

"Oops! Arjun must have given up on me. Let me call him. He said he will take me home. Just now he treats me like delicate china," she laughed.

"You've a wonderful son Anjali, same as you," replied Nalini, happy with her patient's progress. It was time to talk to Arjun about a regular activity which his mother could undertake. She sent him a Whatsapp message to meet her in the clinic same time as the earlier day, along with his father. Whether he liked it or not, Mr Mathur had better be a party to the discussion.

51

Jayant had told his son that he would meet him directly at Dr Singh's clinic at eight pm. He was running late; not that he cared. Always on time for his business meetings, it was on purpose that he was late this evening. He was too irritated with the entire female population just now.

There was Seema who was being difficult since the night of the party. She was too much of a professional for it to show in her work, but their personal relationship was non-existent. Didn't he need her just now, with his wife so ill? Jayant felt sorry for himself.

Then there was this Nalini Singh. What kind of a doctor was she? He had never seen her with a stethoscope. What she did best was talk. She spoke nineteen to a dozen, and he couldn't relate to her.

Jayant was sure by now that Narottam Pai was senile for recommending her so highly. Not at all keen on meeting the psychiatrist, he was going only so as to not upset Arjun. His son had come all the way from England to take care of his mother. And for that too, he had Dr Pai to thank it seemed. Jayant leaned back in the seat of his car, his mind moving fast from one person to another.

Lastly, there was his wife Anjali. Was she really ill? Or was she pretending for want of attention? She had looked so hale and hearty today morning. Was it just six days back that she had fallen at his feet in a dead faint? Could she have feigned that?

A small part of his mind rushed to her defence. He had never seen Anjali ill. In fact, she was the type who was always neatly turned out. She had appeared washed out over the past few days, and she had been too weak to get up. He supposed that she probably was ill. But if that were true, how had she recovered so swiftly with Dr Singh's medication?

It never struck him that Dr Singh had diagnosed Anjali's illness correctly and given her the right medication. It appeared too much of a coincidence to Jayant.

And now the doctor insisted that Jayant visited her clinic along with Arjun once again. He surely didn't want to listen to her scolding voice, her piercing eyes telling him off for being a bad husband. *Arre*! None of them realised that he was the head of a conglomerate with a yearly turnover running to a few billions. One hundred and twenty people worked for him. He had a huge responsibility!

It was a wife's duty to take care of the household and her husband. What was Anjali playing at? Throwing a tantrum just because he had escorted his executive assistant to the party! Men were like that.

By the time Jayant got off at *Athena*, he was in a fuming temper.

52

Nalini sat with Arjun as the two of them discussed how to deal with Anjali's stress. She was happy that her new friend had a strong support in the young man. Her husband was a different ballgame. But she steered her mind away from that thought. It was none of her business how Jayant Mathur lived his life. Right now, Anjali needed to get better, with or without her husband's help.

She looked at Arjun and said, "Your mother is improving by leaps and bounds. Right now, though, it's the medication which is helping her. That will be of no use in the long run. Encourage her to return to her meditation classes for one thing."

"I thought long and hard after meeting you yesterday, Doc. I'll plan a holiday for my parents before I leave. Do you think she'll be fit enough to travel in a month's time?" asked Arjun.

Nalini liked the idea and she nodded, smiling. "That's an excellent plan, Arjun. Consult with her about the trip, ask her where she wants to go, what kind of activities she will be interested in doing there and create a package with her enjoyment being the utmost priority." She met the young man's eyes and knew that he understood what she meant.

Arjun nodded. "Sure ma'am. And another thing you had mentioned is that Mom needs a regular occupation for at least a few hours every day. I think that can be arranged. Let me get more details together before I can say for sure."

"Brilliant, Arjun! That will be a sure-fire cure for your mother's sickness. She needs something to look forward to when she wakes up in the morning. She's extremely intelligent and that needs an outlet."

Her expression tightened the moment Jayant Mathur walked in. Bringing a forced smile to her face, she said, "Hello Mr Mathur, please sit down. Arjun and I were just talking about Mrs Mathur..."

"I think she has recovered from whatever had been ailing her. Thanks! I'm glad she can get back to her regular life," said Jayant abruptly.

"Dad, please. Mom appears alright, but it is temporary. For her to become one hundred per cent mentally fit, she needs to—we all need to, actually—make a few changes to our lifestyle," said Arjun.

Nalini nodded encouragingly, glad to see that the younger man had completely understood what was required to be done.

Jayant frowned heavily, obviously not liking what he heard. "But there's nothing wrong with Anjali. You are all making a mountain out of a molehill. She was absolutely fine today."

"You're right, Dad! But she can't keep taking pills forever. Mom needs a mentally stimulating occupation. She..."

"But what the hell will she do? She's not trained for anything. She's too old to learn." Jayant scowled all the more. "Well, she can come over to my office for a few hours every day. But I don't think she'll like that."

What the hell did he mean that Anjali was too old to learn? Nalini knew of people twenty years her senior who were willing to learn new things. Acquiring fresh knowledge kept a mind healthy and young. Jayant Mathur obviously didn't understand that.

Nalini shook her head subtly when Arjun turned to look at her for guidance. The doctor knew that most of her patient's problem was due to her dwindling relationship with her husband. The trouble was bound to escalate if Anjali encroached on his space.

Arjun shook his head. "No Dad, neither of you will like it. That's not a solution. To begin with, I'm going to plan a holiday for the two of you—for just ten days—ideally in about a month's time. You please check your calendar and tell me when it would be convenient for you. In the meanwhile, I'm looking into a couple of options for Mom to do some regular activity which will interest her."

Jayant sat forward, leaning his elbows on the doctor's table, his chin on his interlocked hands. He looked at the doctor and then at his son and sighed. "Okay! I will tell you tomorrow. But go easy on the activity you are planning for your mother. I need her to be at home to take care of my needs."

Arjun nodded his head vigorously while Nalini swallowed the temper which rose from deep within her. What a selfish bastard! There! It did seem that she had an opinion even if she thought he was none of her business.

A rjun went into his father's room to find him lying on the bed, twiddling with the TV remote. He was surfing news channels and was obviously finding nothing interesting.

"Dad?" said Arjun, sitting on the bed beside his father. "About Mom..."

Jayant frowned. "I agreed to go on that frigging holiday. What more should I do? Do you want me to stop going to work and hold your mother's hand through all her waking hours?" he shouted.

Arjun looked at the older man patiently. It was obvious that Jayant was unhappy with the situation which had got out of hand. His father was used to his mother waiting on him hand and foot. He was the one who was always the centre of attention. Now, his life had gone topsy-turvy and he obviously wasn't liking it.

"Dad! I know you must be upset, Dad. But as you can see for yourself, Mom is getting better. All she needs is an occupation—for about two-three hours in a day. I..."

"What the hell will she do?" Jayant's scowl got blacker.

Arjun put a hand on his father's shoulder, doing his best to calm him down. "Do you trust me to do the best for both of you?" he asked, looking into his father's eyes, willing him to calm down.

Jayant nodded, still looking doubtful, though his frown had turned less ferocious.

Arjun smiled. "I met this author at CCD. He lives in the same complex. He needs someone to do research on the internet, for his next book. I'm sure Mom will be interested and will also be able to manage that. And it won't take too much of her time."

"Hmm!" Jayant rubbed his cheek, obviously wondering how this was going to affect his life. Arjun watched on patiently, confident that he could sway his father to his way of thinking.

"But what about all the work she has at home?"

"What work Dad? Sita *Mausi* does the cooking. Radha does the cleaning. And there are two more people to take care of the rest of the work. What does Mom actually do?" he asked, logically.

"Just because you have moved out of home and don't need your mom to take care of you, it doesn't mean I don't need her, Arjun," said Jayant, his frown growing darker again.

"Dad, let me ask you something straight. What kind of relationship do you have with Mom? Why has she shifted to the other room? Is it because of her illness? But shouldn't you be more supportive during this time? I..."

Jayant jumped up from the bed, his temper blowing out of control. "What do you take me for? You believe I threw her out of the room because she's unwell? Your mother can be such a pain in the ass. I'm sure you don't know that side of her. She shifted to that room a few weeks back and has refused to come back here. How the hell can you hold me responsible for that?"

Arjun noticed that his father refused to meet his eyes during the outburst. There was something fishy about the whole thing and he obviously wasn't going to get the information out of his father.

He got up to go hug his dad. "Calm down Dad! I'm not accusing you of anything. I'm just worried that you both are having problems. And I am so far away. How...?"

Jayant held his son's shoulders and looked at him lovingly. "You are the best thing that's come out of our marriage, my son," he said, before kissing him on his forehead.

Instead of making Arjun happy, his father's words upset him all the more.

So, his mother had shifted out of their room of her own volition. And she definitely must have a reason. Anjali was the most patient and tolerant person he knew. Arjun was sure she would tell him in her own time as she always shared everything with him.

54

Father and son were at Café Coffee Day, when Arjun rose to greet the man walking towards them. Jayant looked up from reading the menu to recognise the man from the Vermas' party, his face turning red with anger. He got up in a hurry, pushing his chair so hard that it fell on its back. Uncaring, Jayant snarled at the man who had danced the evening away with Anjali the other day.

"What the hell are you doing here? Haven't you caused enough trouble between my wife and me?" He wasn't really bothered that there was no logic in his accusation. Jayant didn't like the idea of his wife paying attention to another man, though if he remembered right, the two of them hadn't even talked much. But that still didn't excuse them from monopolising each other. And this man had been responsible for that.

Jayant didn't notice Arjun staring at him, a look of mild shock on his face. "Dad, this is Parth Bhardwaj, the author I spoke to you about."

Jayant didn't take his eyes off Parth. "I don't care if he is the Prime Minister," he snarled. "First and foremost, he's a home-wrecker." He didn't quite know how to tell his young son that the so-called author could be turning his mother's head. Jayant seethed, refusing to acknowledge his son's look of enquiry. He would have to deal with it later.

"Now that you know who I am, let me see. You must be Jayant Mathur, Arjun's father. I have heard a lot about what a great businessman you are. I'm glad to make your acquaintance," said Parth, putting forth his hand.

Jayant ignored the hand in front of him and continued to glower at Bhardwaj. By now Arjun had lifted the chair which had fallen down and set it behind his father.

"Dad, let's all sit down and talk. Please don't be angry."

"You're a kid, Arjun. You don't know this man. He..."

Parth said softly, "I don't quite understand why you are angry with me, Mr Mathur. You..."

Jayant banged a fist on the table. "Don't you? How dare you play the innocent? You were there at the Vermas' party that night, weren't you? You wouldn't let go of my wife. You..."

"Dad!" Arjun's shocked voice interrupted him mid-sentence.

Jayant turned to look at his son, shaking his head. "You don't know anything, Arjun. This man is trying to come between your mom and me." There! He had put it into words. Let Arjun make out what he wanted of it. His mother wasn't exactly the saint he believed her to be.

Parth laughed, shaking his head. "Mr Jayant Mathur, I wouldn't dream of doing that. I met your wife Anjali for the first time that evening. I'd never known her before. Yes, I danced with her. That's only because she's an excellent dancer and no one else seemed ready to partner with me probably because I knew hardly anyone there."

Jayant stared at the man, his temper cooling down somewhat. Anjali had probably remained with the stranger to avoid being questioned about Seema's presence by the other guests. He had been aware of it deep down. And for another, despite all his shouting, Parth Bhardwaj hadn't lost his cool. If he was guilty of what Jayant was accusing, he would have definitely shouted back. "Er..." he looked at the author, really looked at him for the first time. "My son says you are an author. What do you write?" he asked.

"I write thrillers and travelogues," said Parth.

"And what do you do for a living?" asked Jayant, his lip curling. He knew these lazy arty types. They were good for nothing. He felt absolutely no threat now. He was sure Anjali wouldn't have any respect for such a useless guy. His wife wasn't the straying kind anyway. He visibly calmed down, completely convinced now that there was nothing between her and Parth Bhardwaj. It had all been in his mind.

"I get by with what I receive from my publishers," said Parth, a mild smile on his face.

Jayant smiled back, feeling extremely superior. "No hard feelings." That was his way of apologising.

"None at all," said Parth.

Arjun spoke, "Okay Dad, Parth is the author I spoke to you about. He needs someone to do research for his next book. I think Mom will be able to do it. Ask him any questions you need to."

Jayant nodded at his son before turning to look at Parth. "You must understand that Anjali has never worked before. She's a graduate, of course. I wouldn't have married her otherwise, ha-ha! But she has never had to lift a finger in her life. Even now, I can't see a purpose to this. But then, her doctor is insistent." He was careful not to mention 'psychiatrist'. What if the man thought he was hiring a mad woman?

He didn't notice that Parth's smile never reached his eyes as he replied, "What I need is not too difficult, Mr Mathur. Arjun tells me that Mrs Mathur can browse the internet. She just needs to jot down a few points. I won't need her to work for more than two to three hours in a day."

Jayant finished his coffee and said, "That should be fine then. Why don't you come home for dinner tomorrow? You can talk to Anjali then. Better yet, I'll call you as I'm reaching home, and will take you home myself. It would be best if Anjali believed that you and I have become friends." What if his rebellious wife refused to work for the man otherwise? It was best if she believed she was helping out her husband's friend. It never struck him to allow Arjun to deal with the nitty-gritty. He had to be in charge.

They exchanged numbers after Parth nodded once again. Jayant didn't notice Parth winking at his son while Arjun grinned at the author, raising his hand to show him a 'thumbs-up'.

arth watched Arjun go with his father, his smile cynical. Son of a bitch! Mathur had married Anjali only because she was a graduate! He obviously didn't care for her, not as a person in her own right. But then it was obvious that Jayant Mathur was a businessman through and through; what he gained from any scenario counted more than anything else.

He was unfaithful to his wife and he suspected her of betraying him. Amazing! Parth liked both Anjali and Arjun. They were both as honest as anyone can be.

But what about his own motives? Why had he put up with Jayant Mathur's insolence? Parth was never the one to take insults lying down. But today, when Mathur had accused him of turning Anjali's head, Parth had remained cool about it. Why would that be?

He was ready to face anything to get a chance to know Anjali better. There! The truth was out. That was what he wanted—to get closer to her.

But why? It was only the other day that he had decided, firmly, to shut her out of his life. He knew from what she had told him that she wasn't happy with Jayant Mathur. And Mathur apparently didn't care for her either. Otherwise, he wouldn't be involved with his executive assistant. And that woman had not been the first affair either, he was told.

So, Parth looked on it as a heaven-sent opportunity when Anjali's son had approached him. That he genuinely wanted to help the mother-son duo was also true. Having her work for him was an opportunity to find out if there was more to the attraction he felt for her.

Of course, Parth was clear that he would never have an affair with a married woman. But getting to know someone wasn't the same as sleeping with her, right? He could explore if they were mentally attuned to one another. That first evening at the party, he had so enjoyed her presence though they had barely exchanged a few words. The second time they met, he had felt so sorry to hear the horrid life she led of a rich housewife with nothing to do. He was sure she wasn't averse to him either.

Parth had always taken his chances in life and turned up aces. Why not now? He mentally shrugged his shoulders. There was nothing to lose.

56

njali definitely felt more cheerful than before. The medicines had helped her and so had also her newfound friendship with Nalini Singh. But then, the doctor had a busy practice and they couldn't meet as often as Anjali would have liked. Arjun was planning to leave by end of week. It was better that he got back to his studies as soon as possible. He had already missed two weeks' worth of lectures.

But... she did her best to push away the wave of self-pity which threatened to engulf her. There was more than an hour to kill before dinner. Arjun was out meeting his friends. She hoped he would get home before Jayant did. She wanted to spend as less time as was possible with her husband. And even now she made the effort only for her son's sake. If it had been just the two of them, she would have probably had her meal in her bedroom. No, Anjali didn't plan to forgive her husband. Not that he had apologised for his atrocious behaviour.

She walked around the apartment aimlessly, her mind roaming around. Maybe she could read a book. She picked out her favourite novel by Paul

Bainsbridge. She had already read *The Devil's Shadow* twice. The book had never failed to thrill her each time. But today, one face kept interfering as she found herself unable to concentrate. Parth!

How many times should she tell herself that he was out of reach? For one thing, she was married. And for another, she didn't know a damn thing about him. Maybe he was married with a couple of grown up children. Though his apartment had seemed like a bachelor pad, with no feminine touches. But that could mean anything. What if he was gay?

Anjali couldn't help the smile which broke out on her face. Her imagination was truly going haywire. She placed the book on a side table as she stopped pretending to read. She had enjoyed the way Parth had held her—gently, as if she was precious. She had never felt that way in her life. Moreover, she had liked it too much.

A small sigh broke out from Anjali, as she shook her head to herself. What stupidity was this? It was high time she reined in her mind and stopped thinking of Parth. He could never be hers. She felt a pain in the region of her heart when she acknowledged the fact. With firm determination, Anjali got up to go have a shower before dinner. Forget Parth!

Her world turned upside down when the object of her thoughts walked into their apartment with none other than her husband and son. Anjali blanched, unable to fathom the right way to handle the situation. Her heart was in her throat as fine tremors shook her body. She felt hot first and then cold. Would it be obvious to the others?

rjun grinned widely at his mother, completely unaware of the swirling undercurrents. Going forward to hug her, he said, "Mom, you'd never guess who our guest is."

He didn't notice the frustration in her eyes when she turned to him. "I have met Parth," she said softly.

Arjun shook his head at her, his expression turning mischievous.

In the meanwhile, Jayant showed Parth to a sofa, mixed a scotch and soda for him before speaking up, "Yes Anjali, you met Parth Bhardwaj the other day. Are you aware he's a writer?"

Seeing her shake her head, Arjun said, "Mom, I give you three chances to guess Parth's penname. I'm sure you never will."

"Hello Anjali, we meet again." Parth smiled softly.

"Hello! What do you write?" she asked, sitting on a chair in the furthest corner of the living room.

"Thrillers!" answered Parth briefly.

"Mom!" said Arjun. "You love his books, you have read every one of them, at least twice." He felt like a magician on the verge of pulling a rabbit out of his hat.

He saw Anjali looking at the three of them blankly, obviously having no clue to what was coming.

"Mom, Parth Bhardwaj is Paul Bainsbridge," declared Arjun, unable to contain himself. He was thrilled to see his mother's jaw drop open. She would have never guessed in a hundred years.

He was shocked to the core of his being when his mother slid off her chair, in a faint.

"Mom!" he rushed to her, going on his knees beside her. He took a glass of water from the dining table and sprayed a few drops on her face. "Mom," he called out again, shaking her shoulder. He was relieved when she opened her eyes slowly as colour returned to her pale cheeks.

"Did you have your medicines in the afternoon, Mom?" he asked her solicitously. He helped her to her feet when she nodded. Though Dr Singh had warned him this might happen, it had still come as a jolt. "Come on, let's have dinner first. I'm sure you're hungry." He sat his mother on a dining chair. He turned to look at his father and their guest. Their glasses remained untouched as their eyes were focused on his mother. "Do you mind if we start dinner?" At their collective nod, he called out, "Sita *mausi*, please serve the food. We are ready."

58

eing a man of action, Parth found it difficult to hold himself back. He couldn't believe his eyes when he saw Anjali fall down in a faint. Yes, Arjun had told him all about his mother's illness. But to actually see her blacking out in front of his eyes was something else altogether. He paled under his tan, his anger mounting against his host. What man was he, unable to take care of his wife? Why get married at all then? Was being an excellent businessman enough? Did it automatically make him a successful person? Well, it seemed like that was how the world perceived him. An inadvertent sigh escaped Parth as he got up to follow Mathur to the dining table.

It wasn't easy to watch Anjali as she pushed the food around in her plate. He could see that Arjun was an adoring son, at his mother's side, taking care of her. But how could that be enough? Mathur had gone nowhere near her. On one side Parth wanted to hold Anjali close to his person and kiss her worries away. On the other hand, he wanted to sock Mathur, hard. Well, he obviously could do neither as he swallowed the excellent meal which tasted like sawdust to him.

He waited for Mathur or Arjun to introduce the subject of Anjali's job with him as a researcher, in vain. Mathur's concentration was on his plate as he ate his food heartily. While Arjun was ensuring that Anjali ate well.

Parth spoke up suddenly. "Anjali, what do you like about my books?"

He couldn't help noticing the wild expression in the brown eyes which looked at him when she heard him address her. He could see that she was doing her best to smile, but her face refused to cooperate it seemed.

Her "Well," came out huskily before she cleared her throat. "Well, I like your characters and the way you build the scenes, but mostly your language. It's truly convincing. I would never have believed the author wasn't an Englishman if someone else had told me so. I have to confess that I've read your books many times over."

Parth noticed the relief on Arjun's face as he turned to serve some *chicken biryani* on his own plate. Mathur looked up from his plate which was already polished clean, listening to his wife. He didn't join the conversation and Parth noticed there was no mention of Mathur having read his books.

"Thank you," replied Parth, his sharp eyes resting on Anjali as she refused to meet his gaze. "What do you think of the background scenes? Like the description of places and subsidiary characters?" he asked.

A small frown of concentration appeared on Anjali's forehead when she responded, "Authentic is the word which comes to my mind." He noticed that she was eating better, distracted by his talk.

"Well, I'm setting out to pen my next," he said and was gratified to see the enthusiasm on her face.

"Oh really! When will it hit the market?"

"That's still a long way to go. What I'm looking for is someone who will do a bit of research work for me. Like, my story will run across three countries or maybe more by the time I finish it. I need information on the geography, people, clothes, cuisine, famous landmarks, customs and more about those countries. I'm sure you are aware that all this information can be found on the internet," he continued as she nodded, a spark of interest entering her eyes as she looked at him directly for the first time that evening. "Would you be interested in gathering such information?"

Parth was mesmerised when the interest turned to surprise and then delight as she asked, "Me? You want me to do the research for you? Are you sure?" He saw her turn to Arjun, not Mathur, as she asked, "Arjun! Did you hear what Parth said just now? What do you think?"

"It sounds interesting, Mom," drawled Arjun, keeping his enthusiasm to the minimum. "Do you think you can manage? I'm sure Parth will be looking for minute details." He raised an eyebrow as he looked at Parth.

Parth nodded his head. "That's right, I'll need a lot of details. Like when I describe a person or place or a situation, it needs to be realistic. Will you be up to it?" he smiled a genuine smile for the first time that evening, glad to see the cheer on her face.

He saw her eyes dart towards Mathur before she looked at him once again. "I can definitely give it a try, maybe for a month or so. You can always sack me if you find I'm not good enough," she laughed softly, bringing a look of tenderness to Parth's gaze. "By the way, how long do I have to come up with the details? How many hours do you think I'll need to work?"

Parth watched her as she spooned in the last of the *biryani* into her mouth while she waited for his answer. "Probably a couple of hours in a day. It's all flexible. If you work longer hours, you are free to work lesser days. I am thinking in the lines of three to four months for you to get all the matter together. After that, I may require you to look up a few things, just in case they are missed."

"That shouldn't be too difficult. I'm game if you are ready to risk it," she grinned, a mischievous glint in her eyes, reminding him of Arjun.

Parth smiled right back, saying, "You haven't asked the most important question yet."

When Anjali looked at him enquiringly, Mathur interrupted to say, "Yes, the money part. You need to ask Bhardwaj what he intends to pay you for your time and effort." His voice was curt to the point of rudeness, as if he found his wife flighty and foolish.

Parth noticed the smile disappearing from her face as she looked at him and said, "I don't know, Parth. I'd love to do this work. You pay me whatever you think fit. I..."

"That's stupid, Anjali, not at all professional. You need to ask for a specific remuneration before setting to work." Mathur's voice was sharp with censure.

Arjun said, "Dad, I'm sure Mom and Parth can deal with that part. Let us both keep out of it."

Parth pressed his fists hard on his jean-clad thighs, controlling his urge to throw a punch at Mathur with great difficulty. "You'll be paid on an hourly basis, Anjali, whatever the market rate is for this kind of work. We'll review things after a couple of weeks to see if it's working in favour of both of us."

"Of course, and she'll be able to work from home," declared Mathur, a smile on his face.

While Parth had thought along the same lines, Mathur's interference put his back up. And he also caught Arjun shaking his head, his eyes trained on him. Oh yes! Arjun had mentioned that his mother needed to get out of the house more.

His piercing eyes turning on Mathur, Parth said, "That won't be possible. Anjali will need to work with me, at my place. She can have a room to herself, without anyone disturbing her."

Both husband and wife gave him shocked looks—though for entirely different reasons—as if he had just dropped a bomb on them.

59

njali felt shaken. Firstly, Parth Bhardwaj had walked into her home. How the hell was she supposed to forget her attraction for the man? She had been confident that it would go away with time *if* she never saw him ever again. No such luck it seemed.

Over and above that, hearing that he happened to be her most favourite author on earth had been too much to absorb. One minute, she had been sitting there listening to Arjun talk about Parth, the next minute she had blacked out, unable to take the shock of Parth's real identity. Fate seemed to be relentless in making him more and more appealing to her. How was she going to fight it?

Now, all three of them—yes, even Jayant, she was surprised to note—had come up with a plan for her to work with Parth. While one part of her was afraid, she couldn't help being thrilled with the idea. She was scared of working in close proximity with him; but this surely was a heaven-sent opportunity. She would be a fool to miss it. She would get to leave the house every day for a few hours and do something using her brain for a change. She wouldn't dream of missing this opportunity to work on Paul Bainsbridge's next book.

It had been a long time since Anjali felt enthusiastic about something.

60

Jayant saw that Anjali's life was taking a different course from what he had planned. But there wasn't much he could do about it just now. The psychiatrist had insisted that Anjali needed an 'intelligent' occupation, something that would 'interest' her, make her look forward to waking up in the mornings. Yes, she had also reiterated the need for Anjali to spend more time outside the house.

He couldn't understand what was with these modern women. In yonder days, women were happy remaining at home, taking care of their husband and families. Take his own mother for example, her life revolved around his father. What the hell had he done to deserve a wife like Anjali? All these years that he had lived with her, he had never thought of her as a weak person. But even he couldn't deny his shock when she had fainted, not once, but twice, in the span of a few weeks.

When he agreed to this stupid plan of Anjali getting a job, he had been confident that she could do the research from home. Yes, Dr Singh suggested that his wife should go out often. But that didn't mean she had to go to work like a menial, day after day after day. After all, she was the wife of a millionaire businessman. Jayant didn't care for the idea at all.

Now, the bloody author was suggesting that she work from his residence. Okay, he was confident now that there was nothing between Parth and Anjali. Only Jayant wanted his wife at home, at his beck and call.

He frowned heavily at Parth as the author sat with Anjali discussing exactly what he required. He noticed that his wife's face was animated as she listened to him. Maybe, just maybe, there was something that was worth all the changes they were making in their lives.

But that still didn't mean that he liked it!

61

Anjali rang the bell to Parth's apartment at noon the next day. Her upper lip shone with a fine sheen of sweat, while the hand she raised to push a strand of hair behind her right ear trembled. Her heart beat hard in excitement for two reasons—the obvious being that she was thrilled about having an interesting agenda, something which was different from her daily chores or lack of any. The other one—she was too scared to acknowledge it—was working in close proximity to Parth.

Anjali shook her head to clear it, looking at the door. It must have been three minutes since she rang the bell, but no one had opened it.

She raised her hand to ring the bell again, a bit longer this time. After another wait, she decided to ring it just one more time before leaving when the door was jerked open from within and a sleepy voice grumbled, "Who the hell is it at this unearthly hour? I..."

Anjali stared at the man who opened the door to her, her eyes round with surprise. It was Parth, clad in only a pair of boxers, his chest appearing broader than ever, covered with fine dark hair. His usually piercing eyes were not quite alert as it was obvious that he wasn't fully awake. His hair was tousled, giving him a rakish appearance. It took her less than a minute to run her eyes from the top of his head to the tips of his bare toes and her instinct screamed, 'run'. She stood there, staring at him in morbid fascination, not knowing what to do.

"Holy shit!" swore Parth as he opened the outer door. "Come on in. I'm extremely sorry. I went to sleep at six in the morning and…" he shrugged a wide shoulder, turning around, indicating that she followed him.

Anjali shut her eyes in penance for a second only to open them again and stare at his snug butt. Oh my God! What the hell was wrong with her? Why had she dropped to the level of checking out a man's body, that too one with whom she planned to work closely over the next few months? Damn and a double damn!

"Anjali, please have a seat. Give me fifteen minutes and I'll be awake enough to make sense," said Parth, his lips widening in a bright smile, his eyes not ridden of sleep yet. The morning stubble made his teeth shine all the brighter, making him appear younger.

Anjali nodded. "Should I make some coffee?" she enquired. He sure looked like he could do with a strong cup.

"You are an angel!" he declared, pointing a long finger in the direction of his kitchen. "Do you know your way around a kitchen? I have a filter blend. I take milk and sugar in mine. There's an electric coffee maker..."

Anjali turned away from him, not sure if she could look at him for one more second without making a fool of herself. "No worries. You go ahead. I'll manage," she said over her shoulder, walking in a rush to get as far away from him as possible.

He walked into the hall fifteen minutes later, freshly shaved and showered. Anjali shut her eyes to his attractive frame only to open them in a hurry as the smell of his spicy cologne hit her hard. With her eyes closed, her other senses had gone on red alert. And the image of Parth wearing knee length shorts and a t-shirt in navy blue blazed behind her closed eyelids, making her open her eyes in a rush to stare at him. His hair was combed back neatly though an errant lock kept falling on his broad forehead, however many times he pushed it back.

Anjali handed him a mug of coffee, careful not to touch him. His eyes had lost their sleepy look as they prowled over her.

He raised his cup to her in a silent toast before taking a sip, closing his eyes as he savoured the coffee. "Hmm... just what I needed. It's perfect!" he praised, bringing a blush to Anjali's cheeks. She hadn't heard many compliments in her life.

They finished their coffee in silence before Anjali asked, "Breakfast?"

Parth grinned at her. "Spoken like a proper housewife. Not for me. I had something to eat before going to sleep. How about you?"

"I'm good," she replied softly, her face stiff as his lopsided grin churned her insides.

"Is everything okay, Anjali?" he asked, his quicksilver eyes searching her face.

She refused to look at him as she replied, "Of course. I'm really looking forward to begin work."

"Aah work! Sure, we'll start in a minute. But tell me, what's wrong with your health?" he asked, his interest genuine.

How could she tell him that he was one of the main causes for her depression?

arth was thoroughly distracted and he didn't care. It was barely a week since he had completed writing his latest novel and he was in no hurry to begin his next. Having been to most of the countries around the world, he didn't really need someone to do his research for him. That had been just a ruse to help Arjun when the kid had been desperately worried about his mother's health.

And—a long sigh broke out from within him—it had come with a rider, although a delicious one. He got to spend time with Anjali. His strong principles of staying away from a married woman had fallen somewhere by the wayside. He was confident that it wouldn't be long before Anjali got separated from her husband. They were so obviously headed in that direction.

He was all set to pick up the pieces when their marriage fell apart. Of course, he had no evil intentions. Then again, he had no qualms about making Anjali his since her husband didn't seem to value her, at all.

Look at her now, sitting in front of his spare laptop, chewing her luscious lips in concentration as she searched through different websites to garner information for him. Though she had originally knotted her hair and used a clip to keep it in place, soft strands had escaped and danced around her cheeks. Her long eyelashes fanned out on the said cheeks, making him want to touch them, if only to check if they were really as long as they appeared. She was dressed in sunny yellow which made her skin glow.

Parth found her both gorgeous and sexy. A smile lit his features as he pretended to be busy on his laptop at the other end of the work table, while he continued to study her, his eyes glowing with warmth.

Of all the women he had met around the world, how did this one manage to walk into his heart? Yes, that's what she had done. He couldn't but admire her strong nature. Some people would have called her weak, the way she had broken down at the party. But Parth thought otherwise. He had read a lot between the lines when she had described her life to him the other day. It was a wonder that she had bounced back from her depression in barely a couple of weeks and was all set to work for him. She was a woman worth treasuring for sure.

When Anjali raised her head to look at him, he smiled at her. "Lunch?" he asked. He realised that he was smiling way more than usual.

Anjali pushed her chair back and said, "Do you want me to make something? Let me check what's there in your fridge."

Parth shook his head. "You don't get up from your chair. I'll get lunch for us. Just tell me what you want to eat. There's *pasta, pizza, parathas, upma*. Take your pick," he grinned.

"You plan to order from a restaurant?" she asked, her eyes wide.

"Yeah, from Bhardwaj restaurant," he replied, without batting an eyelid. When she gave him a startled look, he said, "So what do you want to eat?"

"*Pasta*."

"*Pasta* it is. It's all vegetarian though," he warned her.

He went to the kitchen and defrosted two batches of pre-cooked *pasta in pesto sauce* in the microwave, before heating them. He didn't notice Anjali following him. "Hey, you stock up on readymade stuff. That's cool!" she said.

Parth turned to look at her as she stood next to the kitchen platform, too far for his liking. He walked up to her and said, "I stock up, yes." His breathing quickened as he stood next to her. He raised a finger to run it over her eyelashes, his touch feather light. When Anjali gave him a shocked look, he said, "I just wanted to see if your eyelashes were for real. They look so lush and long."

He was pleased to note the colour which ran up her cheeks as her eyes closed tightly. Without a pause, he ran his finger over the other eye too, smiling as her lashes fluttered like butterfly wings under his touch. He was sure that she was as aware of him as he was of her.

He handed two plates, forks and spoons to Anjali before taking the hot *pasta* to the breakfast nook at the other end of the kitchen. "Would you like to have some iced tea with your lunch?" asked Parth as he took a glass jug from the fridge. He removed ice from the freezer and added a few cubes to two tall glasses at Anjali's nod. Filling the glasses to the brim with tea, Parth placed them near the plates.

He nodded at Anjali, saying, "Tuck in!"

He sat down once she was settled and began to eat ravenously. When Anjali had a couple of bites, he asked courteously, "How do you like it?"

"It's amazing, Parth. You'll have to tell me where you get your pre-cooked meals from. I'd like to store some at home. Do they last long? The *pasta* tastes so fresh."

Parth laughed, shaking his head. "I did tell you that they are from Bhardwaj restaurant. Once a week, on an average, I turn cook for the whole day. I cook and bake whatever takes my fancy and store the food in a separate freezer."

He was gratified to see Anjali's mouth fall open while her fork clattered to the floor.

ven before Anjali could get off the bar stool to pick up her fork, Parth was there, on his haunches, his silver gaze studying her intensely. She refused to meet his eyes as he handed her the fork. She felt an electric shock when he touched her hand, her face going pale. He was still on his knees, his head on a level with the table, as she looked down at him from her high perch. With great difficulty, she controlled the urge to push back the lock of hair which fell on his forehead.

"Anjali." His voice was compulsive, his hand holding her wrist in a loose grip.

"Mmm." No, she refused to look at him or she wouldn't be responsible for what she might do. The next second, she was startled to find Parth standing next to her, his hand cupping her right cheek.

Giving him a shocked look, Anjali said, "Parth, what are you doing?"

"You tell me. What are you doing to me, Anjali?" he came back, tracing the shape of her lips with his thumb, an expression of intense concentration on his face.

Anjali shook her head, her hand closing over his wrist, trying to pull his hand away from her face. Only there was no strength in the fingers which encountered his skin. Her fingers traced the fine hairs on his wrist, while her thumb couldn't help but feel the pulse. It beat rhythmically against her finger, making her more aware of him than ever before.

It felt as if he was weaving a cocoon of magic around her. She wanted to simply shut her eyes and give herself up to his caresses.

"Parth!" her voice was choked.

"Anjali..." he whispered close to her ear, his hot breath stirring her nerve-ends. Her eyes shut in surrender when she felt his lips press against her temple. She felt him lift her from her seat and stand her on the floor, his arms going around her waist.

"Parth, this is not right," she protested, her heart not really in it.

"Just one kiss," he said, "I promise not to ask for more."

Anjali's protest died on her lips when he kissed the corner of her mouth, his tongue darting out to taste her. Parth made his move when her jaw dropped in alarm, his lips settling on hers in a deep kiss.

Anjali was too caught up in the kiss to realise that she had put her arms around Parth's neck to bring his head closer to hers. When his tongue pushed against her teeth, she welcomed him, going on tiptoe to get closer.

She knew not for how long they were locked in each other's arms when she felt Parth's hold loosen. She held on to him tightly, not wanting to let go.

"Sweetheart, your cell is ringing," he said.

Anjali came back to earth with a crash, a deep sigh issuing from the core of her being. She removed her arms reluctantly and moved away a few inches when he finally let her go. By now, her phone had gone silent. She still refused to meet Parth's intent gaze.

What must he think of her? That her morals were as bad as her husband's?

"Hold that thought," said Parth, as if he could read her mind. "I know enough about you and your marriage to Mathur to understand that you have always remained loyal to him. And I have too much respect for you."

Her brown eyes connected with his silver gaze then. "Parth, I... I don't quite know what came over me. I...," she bent her head, feeling ashamed of herself. How could she crave Parth's kisses so?

"There's nothing abnormal about what you are feeling, Anjali." He reached a hand to caress her cheek.

Without meaning to, Anjali pressed her cheek into his hand as she thought, *it's all very well for you to say that. But in the eyes of the world, what I am doing is wrong.* Which still didn't stop her from turning around to press her lips to his palm.

It was a big wrench when Anjali left his arms and home after being kissed so thoroughly. Yes, Parth had kept his promise of not asking for more than one kiss. But that didn't bind her, nor did it stop her from kissing him with fervour, more than once.

Arjun stepped out of Cox and Kings, a wide smile on his face. He had pinned his father for dates and finally booked both his parents on a trip to Greece, and he was glad that his mother had been enthusiastic, planning her tour along with him. Of course, the actual trip would be a month later, just as Dr Singh had advised.

He had also booked his ticket to England for the day after tomorrow. Now that his mother had started working with Parth and was on the road to recovery, it was high time he went back to university.

He reached home at about 4.30 and went directly to give the good news to his mother. She was sitting at the window, appearing distracted.

"Mom!" he called out. "How was your first day?"

"Arjun!" she turned, a smile on her face. Looking closely, he noticed that it didn't reflect in her eyes.

"You didn't enjoy your work?" he asked, his voice anxious.

Anjali smiled. "I loved it Arjun. Sit down *na*. Shall I get you something? Coffee or lemonade?"

"Sita *mausi* is bringing coffee for both of us," said Arjun. Just then Sita entered. He took the tray from her and placed it on a side table. Once she was out of the room, he asked, "Tell me more." He gave a mug to his mother before settling on the window seat beside her with his own.

"When do you plan to go back to college? I hope you aren't going to hang around for long. You know I am fine now. You must book your return..."

"Whoa!" grinned Arjun. "I can see that you can't wait to be rid of me. I'm leaving on the day after tomorrow. In the meanwhile, I have organised the bookings for your and Dad's trip to Greece. I don't know about him but I know that you'll surely love it."

What he didn't expect was the smile to disappear from his mother's face.

"Arjun, I've been wanting to talk to you. I don't think I want to be your father's wife anymore. Will you forgive me?" she asked, her voice shaking with emotion. But her eyes remained dry.

Though her words didn't entirely surprise Arjun, it still disturbed him. He put his coffee cup aside to hug his mother.

"I understand, Mom. You aren't happy with Dad. I have kind of been aware of it for a long time. Whatever your decision is, I'm with you." He held her close.

"Thank you, Arjun. You're the best thing which has happened out of our marriage. Hey, what are you grinning about?" she asked, an answering smile stretching her lips wide.

"Dad said the same thing a few days back. That's what made me smile."

"*Chalo*, that's at least one common ground between us," she replied, without rancour. "It has been a farce Arjun, for many years. I won't blame your father entirely. It's just that we have moved too far apart. And thank you so much for accepting my decision."

"I only want the two of you to be happy, Mom. If separation is what it takes to be happy, so be it," he said, way wiser than his years.

"I'm sorry you booked a trip for us. I don't think it's the right time."

"I'd still give it a try Mom. You need a holiday and it will do Dad a lot of good too. Maybe this trip will help heal your wounds. Not that I'm suggesting it will help you get back together, only so that you don't hold each other in anger and dislike."

"You sure have grown up a lot, my son," said Anjali, kissing him on his forehead.

njali had been expecting his call, dreading it as well as welcoming it. "Hi Parth!" she whispered into her cell phone.

"Hey, where are you? I've been waiting for you since half an hour. Missing you, sweetheart," he said, making her feel all hot and bothered.

"Don't, Parth, please."

"Don't what? Wait for you or miss you?" he asked, tender amusement in his voice.

Anjali couldn't help smiling at his words. "Parth!" she tried to censure him.

"Come on over and we can discuss it over a cup of coffee and the choco chip cookies I baked late last night."

Temptation, thy name is Parth.

"Promise me that we'll only talk," she said, worrying her lower lip.

"Where are you?" he asked, not answering her question.

"In the garden below your building."

"What are you doing there when you should be working? Won't your boss be angry?"

"Parth, how I wish he would; be angry with me, I mean. I'm scared, Parth," she whispered, worry eating into her.

"Of what, sweetheart? Of me?"

She shook her head vigorously. Realising that he couldn't see her, she said, "Not of you, Parth. I'm scared of myself. I..."

"Will you please come over now? Or do you want me to come and get you?" He sounded urgent.

"I'm coming," she said, cutting his call.

She walked into his penthouse a few minutes later, her heart beating hard. She shut the door behind her, following the smell of coffee and chocolate.

"Mmm... something smells divine," she said, closing her eyes and taking a deep sniff. She was terrified of what he would read in her eyes.

"Open your mouth," said his voice close to her ear, his breath on her cheek, though he never touched her.

Anjali obeyed him as he fed a piece of cookie into her mouth, his fingers brushing against her lips. She munched on it, enjoying the flavour. But her throat wouldn't let her swallow comfortably. Her eyes teared up as she desperately looked around for some drinking water.

"Was it that bad?" he asked, surprise in his voice as he handed her a bottle of water.

Anjali drank a few gulps before answering him. "Of course not, Parth, and you very well know it."

"Hmm." His eyes roved over her face hungrily. "You mean it just went down the wrong way?" he asked, persistent.

She wouldn't meet his gaze. "Where's the coffee you promised me?"

"In the living room," he gestured, continuing to study her.

"Why are you looking at me like that? Do I have crumbs on my face?" she asked, desperate for him to switch his attention elsewhere. But she succeeded in only having him move closer in the pretext of checking her face for crumbs.

"Only on your lips," he replied, bending down suddenly and licking them away. "There, you're clean now."

Anjali raised shocked brown eyes to his silver gaze. But she refused to rise to the bait as she walked to the living room and plopped down on a sofa.

"Do you really think we can work together?" she asked.

"I don't see a problem," he said, taking a sip from his coffee mug. Thank God he was sitting on the opposite side, facing her.

"Parth, I'm asking you seriously." Her eyes begged him for she knew not what.

Parth sighed. "I'm not joking either. You have nothing to fear from me, Anjali. Yes, I like you tremendously, maybe more than that. But I'll never make any demands on you which you are not ready for."

"Do you realise that it's not you I'm afraid of? How could I be? You are the one who offered me the solace I've never found in my life. I don't fear you, Parth. I'm scared of myself, of this powerful feeling of... of... lust

I have for you." There! She had finally given a label to what she felt for him. Wasn't it the truth? If it was shameful, then too bad!

"Anjali." Parth was beside her the very next second. He removed the coffee mug from her nerveless fingers and pulled her into his arms, pressing her face into his shoulder. "You poor sweetheart! Don't feel so terrible. Is it so bad to lust after me?"

No, he wasn't laughing at her. But the tender amusement she had sensed before was back in his voice. He was too damn irresistible.

She held on to him tightly, her arms around his waist. "Please Parth! Save me from myself," she whispered, agony in her voice.

It took a while, but she calmed down with the rhythmic stroking of his large hand down her back.

arth's heart brimmed with love for the woman in his arms. And how could he not love Anjali? He had never met a more honest person in his life. He needed to remember that she was recovering from depression and should go easy on her. Arjun had trusted him to give her a job and here he was, flirting with her at every opportunity. It just wasn't done!

He removed his arms from around Anjali, but continued to sit next to her. "Do you feel better?" he asked gently.

Anjali nodded, looking more peaceful than when she had entered his apartment.

"Let me get us some fresh coffee. And after that, let's get cracking. We need to get a lot of work done," he said, getting up. He missed having her in his arms, but no way was he going to give in to temptation. He needed to be the stronger person here.

And that was how he let her work at one end of the table, continuing to study her from the other end. *Patience* was his second name. He would wait for her to recover from her illness and then woo her away from her meaningless marriage. Anjali deserved to be happy.

Of their own volition, Parth's fingers began to type on his laptop as he breathed life into his latest heroine.

67

"If you weren't keen to go on the trip, why did you make a promise to Arjun?" asked Anjali, her voice trembling with disillusionment and her escalating temper. She was extremely disappointed when Jayant insisted that it wouldn't be possible for them to go to Greece. Despite the chasm looming between the two of them, she had been looking forward to the trip. It was so unfair that Jayant wanted to cancel it now, at the last moment.

Jayant shrugged. "I did try telling Arjun that I might be busy. But he was too insistent. At that point I felt I could manage to get away, which is why I gave him those dates. But the most unexpected has happened. I'm expecting a delegation from Australia who will be visiting our office as well as the factory. I can't let someone else deal with them."

That was all! No apology. But then that was how it had always been, through the couple of decades of their married life.

Anjali's mind worked furiously. What if she went on the trip by herself? She was planning to leave Jayant anyway. She was just waiting to recover fully before trying to fathom what she wanted to do with her life and where she wanted to live, once she left him. Maybe this would be the first step to gain independence.

"You cancel your ticket. I will continue with my plans," she declared.

"What?" yelled Jayant, "Have you gone mad? You wouldn't be able to manage a day there by yourself. How the hell...?"

"I will!" she said quietly, a mutinous set to her chin. "If college girls can manage to go alone on trips, I most definitely can."

Jayant glared at her. "Don't be an idiot, Anjali. Let's both go next month. I promise..."

She smiled without rancour. She knew his promises of old, but that was not the reason for her smile. She was thinking of Parth and his promises. "Forget it, Jayant! We both know that you are married to your business. I don't expect more from you. You do your job. I'll go and play the spoilt, rich wife which you keep accusing me of."

She could see that he didn't like it. But then, what could he do?

Jayant called their son. "Arjun, will you please talk sense to your mother? She has gone crazy," he declared, without preamble.

He gave the phone to Anjali, a smug expression on his face.

Anjali said, "Hi Arjun! Is it a good time to talk? Or are you busy?" She was smiling and it showed in her voice.

"Hello Mom! You're sounding good. My lectures for the day got over some time back. Tell me, why have you gone crazy?" he asked, an answering grin in his voice.

"I'm off to Greece on my own as your father's too busy to take off," she said. She ignored Jayant as he kept shouting in the background.

"But that's great, Mom. I'm so glad you aren't cancelling your trip. I had booked it especially for you. Please go and have fun. Maybe I can take a couple of days off and join you on one of your day tours. What say?!" he asked enthusiastically.

"That would be perfect, Arjun. Do that! I've been so looking forward to visiting Greece. It's barely for ten days. Since the round trip is booked, there's absolutely no worry. I'll be a pampered lady," she laughed.

Jayant snatched the phone from her hand and snarled, "Arjun, have you also taken leave of your senses like your mother? She cannot go on her own. I will not allow it."

Anjali watched on as father and son argued for the next twenty minutes. She wasn't bothered. Her husband had lost his stranglehold on her. It might take time for him to realise that, but she had been aware of it over the past many weeks.

Jayant looked drained after the conversation with their son. He glared at her saying, "You do whatever the hell you want. Don't blame me if something goes wrong. A man needs his peace. How the hell will I do business otherwise? And if I don't work, where will the money come for you to splurge?"

"I won't," said Anjali firmly, pleased to see the startled expression on his face. "Blame you, I mean. And nothing will go wrong. You please continue to take care of your business, in peace."

68

The moment his father disconnected the call, Arjun called Parth.

"Hi Arjun, how are you doing?" asked Parth. The two of them had been in regular touch, their common concern for Anjali bringing them close.

"Just awesome, Parth. And you?" he asked. He felt a deep attachment to the older man. He also knew that his mother admired Parth a lot, and not just as a writer. Arjun could garner that from the way she spoke about her job and the time she spent in Parth's home.

"I'm doing good, sonny. And how's your Jane? Running circles around you yet?" he teased.

"She tries, of course," said Arjun, grinning. "Listen! May I ask you a favour? I'm already taking advantage of your goodness. I..."

"Get on with it, man! What do you want?" asked Parth affectionately.

"Dad cancelled his Greece trip. But Mom's keen on going. And I think she should. I just wanted to ask you something which I can't ask anyone else. Do you think she's fit to go by herself? Three months back,

I wouldn't have been bothered. But with her recent illness, I feel a mite worried."

"Shit! The bastard! Why does he make promises which he doesn't mean to keep?" He went silent for a few seconds before saying, "Oh God! I'm sorry Arjun. I'm truly sorry. Please forget that you heard me say that. That was truly dumb of me."

Arjun smiled sadly. "That's alright, Parth. I suppose I can't complain as your anger is on my mother's behalf. My father isn't all that bad, Parth. Only they both are poles apart."

"You noticed that too," stated Parth.

"Since a long time. I'll let you in on something else too. My Mom wants to go separate."

"How do you know? Did she tell you that?" asked Parth.

"Yes, even before I returned to England. And I agree that she needs a life of her own."

"She must be truly proud to have you for her son, Arjun. And thank you for letting me know, buddy. Will you mind awfully if I go to Greece with your mother? Let me be straight with you. My intentions are honourable. I want to spend time with your mother, get to know her on a personal level. I hope..."

Arjun hooted with joy. "Are you serious? You like Mom?"

"Not just like, I love Anjali."

69

Arjun chatted some more with Parth before disconnecting the phone, getting on his cycle to ride to his apartment. Jane was busy most evenings with the part time job which she had refused to give up. He had a lot of time to think as he made dinner, even while loud music played in the background.

Chopping his way through a small mound of vegetables, Arjun's mind went back to his conversation with Parth, that too soon after his argument with his father about Anjali going to Greece on her own.

Deep down, Arjun had been worried that his mother might not be fit enough to travel alone. But then, it was her bid for independence and it wouldn't be fair to stop her. Jayant had been angry, not keen to let his wife go on her own, leaving her precious husband alone. His father had insisted that he would feel lost without his wife. While his mother was actually planning to leave her husband forever. Arjun felt that someone had to take a stand, which was the reason why he had taken Anjali's side. After all, it wasn't fair to her to simply cancel the trip only because his father was too busy to go. Arjun knew only too well that it would be difficult for Jayant to find any kind of free time. He thrived on his business and simply hated being away from it for more than a couple of days at a time. He, Arjun, should have foreseen this before booking the tickets for their trip.

Arjun loved his father, there were no two ways about it. But it had become more and more obvious to him that he wasn't a suitable partner for his mother. Jayant was patriarchal to the core while Anjali was an independent woman. Okay, maybe only in her mind; while physically, she had bound herself to her husband and child. She had been an obedient wife and a loving mother all these years, accepting her role. But now, with her son away from home, she had a lot of time on her hands. While his father spent most of his waking hours at work.

He could very well understand how bored his mother must be, with nothing to do. And no one could deny that she was intelligent and well-read. The excessive idle time on her hands had only driven her to depression. No way was Arjun going to let her slide back into it.

If leaving her husband was the only way for her to be happy, then that's what she must do.

As their son, he could see both sides of the picture. After all, didn't both their blood run in his veins? His father will survive, with or without his mother. He still had his successful business which took most of his attention.

What would happen at the most? Jayant would be like a bear with a sore head for a while, until the time he accepted that Anjali was not going to get back to him. He would settle down after that.

As for his mother, Arjun smiled softly as he stir-fried the veggies, it looked like she had one more person who seemed to love her. A man who could be her partner, unlike her son, who could support her only so much.

Parth was a strong man, silently supportive. Arjun had realised that it must have taken a lot for Parth to keep quiet when his father had insulted him so badly that first day when the three of them met at CCD. It was obvious to him now that the author must have put up with all that only for Anjali's sake.

And Arjun had seen the effect of Parth's adulation on his mother. Within a couple of days of going to work for him, Anjali had undergone a tremendous transformation. He didn't know whether his mother had any deep feelings towards Parth. But he knew for a fact that she admired him as an author and appreciated him as a friend.

But Parth loved her and that was something Arjun felt grateful for. He whistled cheerfully along with the music as he transferred the cooked veggies into a bowl, placing a few slices of bread and butter on a tray before carrying the lot to the dining nook.

If his mother and Parth got together just as Parth hoped, it would make him very happy. Arjun switched off the music before turning on the TV to catch his favourite programme, feeling as if a great weight had been lifted off his chest. While he had been thinking of persuading his mother to move to London with him when she left his father—at least until the time he completed his studies—he had still been a mite worried if Anjali would agree to the suggestion. But now, it looked like Destiny had a better plan for his mother.

Arjun sat back to relish his dinner as he watched the show.

njali was super excited as she checked into her Etihad flight to Athens. It was six in the evening and she decided to get a spa treatment which was included in her first-class ticket.

After an hour and a half, she stepped out of the spa completely rejuvenated and all set for her holiday. An Etihad attendant guided her to a special dining room where she enjoyed a glass of red wine along with a delicious snack. She ran through the travel brochure from Cox and Kings for the fifth time, relishing the thought of visiting all those places she had only read about.

Her flight was called and she walked forward eagerly. She didn't have to wait in a queue as she received nothing short of royal treatment as she was shown into her suite. There was a comfortable single sofa, a vanity unit and a wide couch which turned into bed at night. Luxury indeed! She felt rather sorry for Jayant who really didn't know what he was missing.

There was a flurry of activity when someone got settled in the suite right next to hers. Anjali sighed. She hoped that whoever it was, he wouldn't disturb her.

If Jayant had been with her, she wouldn't have been worrying about it.

Anjali shook her head to herself. She had to stop thinking this way as she planned to leave her husband and lead an independent life. And of course, travelling would play a major part in her future. Smiling to herself, she turned to look out of the window.

"Surprise!" said a husky voice, not far from her.

"Parth!" Colour bloomed on Anjali's face when she saw him stepping into her suite. "What are you doing here?"

Parth shrugged. "What do you think? I'm going to Greece with you."

Anjali stared at him with a sparkle in her eyes. Was he looking uncertain? Parth—the supremely confident author, the one who wove spells with his words—looked unsure of himself.

She grinned at him. "Oh Parth! That's the best news I've heard since ever," she said, rushing headlong into his arms.

71

Parth held her close, pressing his chin to the top of her head, inhaling deeply. Her head barely reached his chest while she had her arms wound tight around his waist.

The past one month hadn't been easy while he had kept his distance, waiting for her to recover from her bout of illness. He hadn't wanted her to feel torn between being Jayant's wife and feeling attracted to another man.

Now that she was clear that she wanted to separate from Mathur, there was nothing to stop him from wooing her. And woo her he planned to do. He knew that her marriage had been arranged and there was no love lost between the two even from the beginning. Anjali needed to know how precious she was and Parth intended to show her over the rest of their lives.

The fingers of his right hand nestled in her hair as he cupped a cheek with his palm, his thumb pressing against her chin to bring her head up. He pressed his lips to her forehead in a gentle kiss. "Anjali."

Anjali went on tiptoe to press her lips to his clean-shaven cheek, inhaling his cologne deeply. "I'm so thrilled to have your company during this holiday. I was feeling so lonely till now."

Parth captured her lips in a mind-blowing kiss, revelling in the softness of her slender frame. His tongue was relentless, exploring her mouth and he was absolutely pleased with her passionate response.

Lifting his head, he grinned at Anjali before settling on the wide single sofa in her suite and pulling her down into his lap. "Have you ordered dinner? They serve some fabulous *a la carte* on the flight, and I'm famished." he said.

"You've been on Etihad before? This is my first trip with the airline. I didn't know about that."

Parth placed the menu in her hands. "Do you mind if we order now? I've not had anything since breakfast."

"Oh! But why Parth?" she asked, staring at his rugged face with her wide eyes.

"Ensuring that I got on the same flight as you, took up all my time. It was only yesterday that I got to know that you were travelling alone," he said, kissing her on the tip of her nose.

"Oh! And how did you know that?" She hadn't mentioned to Parth that Jayant had ditched her yet again.

"Okay, confession time," declared Parth. "Arjun told me. Before you ask, yes, we have been in touch. I'm sure you can guess why."

"Arjun has been talking to you. Why am I not surprised! He's a lot like me. We tend to get along with the same people. I..."

"You find me irresistible and your son simply adores me," said Parth, tongue-firmly-in-cheek, though his eyes were devouring her. His smile turned into a grin when Anjali looked down at the menu, unable to meet the heat in his gaze.

"Do you want to choose for me Parth? I'm not sure I understand half of what's written here." She looked so appealing, her lower lip caught between her teeth as she tried to read the menu.

"Sure, and the next time, I'll show you how to fathom what's there," he said before ringing the bell for a stewardess.

It had been two days since they had arrived in Athens. Both the days, they had rushed around touring the Acropolis and the ancient Agora, while they had also managed to spend a few hours at the National Archaeological Museum.

Feeling beat, Anjali requested to dine in-house at Hotel Grande Bretagne, where they were put up in adjoining rooms. After chilling for over an hour at the rooftop bar which offered a stunning view of the Acropolis, they decided to get room service for dinner.

Parth left Anjali at her door, saying, "I'll see you in a few minutes. Order what you like best. I'll go along with your choice," he winked at her.

Anjali walked into her room, leaving the door unlocked. She didn't plan to get up once she plopped down on the sofa. Her feet were killing her. She sighed softly, a happy smile on her face. No, she wasn't complaining. She was having the time of her life. Parth was such fun to be with and her worry of what he might demand from her had never materialised. Though she so enjoyed his kisses, she wasn't quite ready to jump into bed with him.

She reached for the room service menu and placed her order—a bottle of chilled white wine and a few dishes she was familiar with and also liked. She ordered *kolokythokeftedes* for starters—deep fried patties made from grated courgette which had an amazing flavour. It was served with *tzatziki*—a refreshing combination of yogurt, cucumber, and garlic which Anjali found irresistible. She ordered *moussaka* for the main course. The baked dish came layered with aubergine, minced meat, tomato puree and onion with yummy local spices. Better yet, it was topped with loads of cheese and a mouth-watering sauce unique to the region. The garlic bread which they served with it was the freshest she had ever tasted. And of course, one can't but have a dessert to accompany dinner during a holiday for sure. What better than *baklava,* drenched in honey! She had fallen in love with the flaky pastry crammed with crunchy pistachios.

Order placed, Anjali kicked off her shoes, raised her legs and placed them on a side table, groaning as she settled back into a comfortable position. She pulled down her red knee-length dress which had ridden up, as far as it would go. She was still getting used to wearing western clothes. Though it was pretty decent, she wasn't used to showing so much leg. But right now, she felt too comfortable to change.

"Come in," she called out when she heard a knock on the door.

Parth walked in, a single red rose in his hand. She had still not recovered from seeing him in a tuxedo. He looked impossibly attractive. He presented the rose to her with a wide smile on his face. "Your muscles protesting too much?"

Anjali nodded, her eyes clinging to his, a finger inadvertently caressing the rose. "Give me a moment," said Parth, walking into her bathroom. He came back with a bottle of body lotion and a towel. Sitting cross-legged on the carpet near her feet, he spread the towel on his lap.

"But why Parth?" The words died on Anjali's lips when she felt him lift her right leg off the table to place it on the towel.

Silence reigned in the room as Parth set out to work meticulously. He poured some lotion into his hands and massaged her leg, his touch gentle but firm. Anjali couldn't help the half-sigh, half-moan of pleasure which rushed up from deep within her. It was pure bliss as he gave her a foot massage which she would never forget for life.

She felt pampered as he stroked her legs from the knees down. Her calf muscles felt glorious under his constant kneading. *Have I died and gone to heaven?* thought Anjali as she closed her eyes and gave herself up to his ministrations.

She woke up with a start when she felt Parth's hand on her shoulder. He looked apologetic when he said, "Our dinner's here."

73

Parth couldn't take his eyes off Anjali. Her eyes were smudged with sleep though she chatted her way through dinner. She was probably working hard at staying awake, he thought, amused. "I'm so sorry that I went to sleep Parth. But I've never experienced such a fabulous leg massage ever in my life," she smiled shyly at him. "Don't you feel tired after all that running around?"

Parth shook his head. "Nope! I run ten km, at least five days in a week."

"You do?" her eyes rounded in surprise. "How do you find the time for it?"

He grinned. "I manage."

"You write, you cook and now I know you are a fitness freak. What else? I suppose you studied from a posh hostel. That's where boys learn the value of cooking."

"Did Arjun go to a hostel?" he asked, his eyes dancing with mischief.

Anjali couldn't help her answering smile as she shook her head. "I'm sure you know he didn't."

"Exactly."

"Where did you learn your excellent language skills? Did you go to Oxford?" she asked, curious. He never spoke much about himself.

Parth laughed, shaking his head.

"Then you must have definitely done your post-grad from St. Xavier's in Mumbai," she declared.

"Will you be too appalled if I say I didn't go to school beyond Std. VII?" he asked.

Her big brown eyes went wide in shock as she stared at him. "You are joking!"

He searched her eyes, looking for signs of judgement. There were none. With a sigh and shake of his head, Parth said, "I ran away from home when I was eleven. We lived in Dharavi those days. My father was a daily labourer and my mother used to work as a housemaid." He was neither ashamed nor proud as he uttered the words; just the bare facts. "I am the eldest of four. It was a difficult time, though my parents were insistent about getting us educated. I hated school. I resented the kids who came in cars, carrying fancy school bags and water bottles. There was this fire burning within me. I had to grow beyond all that. Feeling smothered by the four walls of the tiny chawl we lived in, I ran away after school one day."

Anjali stared at him, forgetting the dessert. "And?" she egged on.

Parth grinned reminiscently. "I'm glad I did what I did. If I had really thought about the horrors of fending for myself, I would have never left the safety of my home. But determined brat that I was, I refused to acknowledge defeat when I went hungry on many days. The greatest plus was that I was ready to work hard at anything which came my way. After hanging out near the sea, I stowed away on a fishing trawler. It was only after it reached Goa, did I know its destination. I cleaned and served at small restaurants. Then with the help of some foreigners, I managed to get a menial position on one of the foreign ships and sailed away, never looking back."

Anjali nodded again, no words coming out of her open mouth, astonishment on her face.

"One thing I always loved was reading. I used to work most of my waking hours, but made it a point to read at least four hours every day. I foraged the library on board the ships I worked. Reference books, dictionaries, thesaurus, you name it and it was available. Once the Captain of the first ship became aware of my thirst for knowledge, he granted me special permission to spend time in the library. He even gave me a reference to use on board the next ship, when I left their employ after three years."

"How did you become Paul Bainsbridge?" she asked, awed.

Parth grinned. "Nine years ago, I penned my first novel. I was travelling around Europe then. I tried publishing my book, but there were no takers. That's when I got myself an English agent. Stuart was impressed with my work. But he was also practical. He pitched it to a publishing house in the name of Paul Bainsbridge after consulting with me. Of course, you must have guessed that the initials stand for my own name. It immediately clicked and my first bestseller went to the printers in barely six months."

"What a success story—from the slums of Dharavi to Hiranandani Gardens via the globe! I am truly amazed."

Mild colour ran up Parth's lean cheeks as he took her hand in his. "Anjali."

"So, where's your family nowadays? Did you get in touch with them at all?"

"But of course. I started sending money home when I began earning more than what I needed. Though I met them only two years ago when I returned to Mumbai for the first time since I left."

"They must have found it difficult to even recognise you," said Anjali.

Parth shrugged. "Not really! I look exactly like my father. But then, it did seem like meeting strangers. I'm related to them by blood. But I can't feel a connection."

He didn't mention that he had ensured they all lived a comfortable life in their own homes in high rises. But then, he had too much while they had too little.

"Enough of me now. You tell me something. Do you want to do the arranged tour tomorrow or are you open for some adventure?" he challenged her.

Anjali looked at his eyes which had turned mischievous. "Adventure as in? You mean clambering over rocks?" She shook her head. "I don't think I'm fit enough for that kind of adventure."

Parth shook his head. "I mean a local tour on feet without following the tourist agenda."

"How would you know what to do?"

"Maybe because I know Athens like I know the back of my own hand?" he quipped.

Anjali's mouth fell open once again in the span of an hour. "Is my job with you a farce, Parth?" she got up from her chair and walked up to him, a threatening expression on her face.

Parth got up too. "Of course not…" Before he could complete what he was saying, a tiny tornado rammed into him, raining blows on his person, wherever she could reach.

"You made a fool of me. You don't need anyone to do research for you. You…"

Parth laughed at her puny efforts, taking her fists in his hands. "Listen Anjali, I wasn't fooling you. Yes, the truth is that I could have managed the research on my own. But," his voice rose, to stop her from interrupting, "but, how much ever a writer knows about a place, it's better to have all the small details on paper so that mistakes don't happen. When I take you sightseeing tomorrow, I'll be your guide and do an excellent job of it. But that's only because I will be able to recall stuff as and when I see them. But while writing, chances are high that I might mix up the descriptions of two different European cities. Does that make sense?"

Anjali stared at him for a few seconds before nodding slowly. "Aren't we modest!" she teased.

"So, are we on for tomorrow?" he asked, speaking softly into her ear, before pressing his lips to her hot cheek. He was still holding her hands in his.

Anjali nodded, freeing her hands to throw her arms around his neck. "Parth! Are you aware that you are turning my head, completely?"

74

Jayant was in a fuming temper when he reached his office. Although he would never admit it even to himself, he missed Anjali. It was four days since she left on her holiday and his life at home had fallen apart. He just didn't know how to manage his clothes and shoes. Having a cook and three servants was obviously not enough. He was as helpless as a baby. But did that mean he felt grateful to Anjali for being there for him all the time? Not at all! He was burning with anger and resentment that she had just upped and left him to fend for himself.

The first person who caught his eye was Seema. He walked into his cabin and dialled her extension immediately. "Come here," he barked into the phone before placing the receiver back on the hook.

Seema knocked on his door before walking in. She looked svelte in narrow black trousers and a white formal blouse. His eyes ran over her figure from top to toe, making her blush. He got up from his chair, locking the door with a remote. "Seema," he whispered, standing close to her. He had missed their closeness and having sex with her. Now was the best time to set right their relationship, with Anjali so far away. "I have missed you."

When Seema tried to step away from him, Jayant put his arms around her and held her firmly, letting her feel his arousal. "Wait for me in the evening. We have a date."

When she shook her head, he pressed his lips to the pulse beating at her neck, nuzzling her. "I'm not taking 'no' for an answer."

Jayant was in a better mood after Seema left a few minutes later. He went about his work as usual, waiting for five pm to arrive. He pinged Seema on her cell phone to be ready to leave before packing his laptop into his briefcase.

Whistling under his breath, Jayant left work for the day, tapping Seema's shoulder on his way out. She followed him almost immediately after and the two went to the company's service apartment to spend some quality time together.

Jayant wallowed in self pity as he complained non-stop about his errant and shrewish wife; how she refused to respect her husband, not understanding his needs, so on and so forth. Seema nodded in understanding. He was glad that he had found a sympathetic shoulder to cry on and continued in the same vein as they drank peg after peg of scotch.

With all that alcohol floating around, neither of them noticed that they forgot to use a condom that night.

75

rjun was in constant touch with both his mother and Parth. When he realised that they were having such fun in Athens, he decided not to join them.

"Hey Arjun, we'll be heading home in five days. When do you plan to come over?" asked his mother. Her voice sounded so young and carefree that he felt so happy for her.

"I'm sorry, Mom. I need to complete three different projects and I'm already running late. Please don't mind. But tell me, how's it going?"

"I am having the time of my life, Arjun. Yesterday, Parth took me around the city, showing me the sights. We had some potent Ouzo at a local taverna. I got drunk with barely a few sips. Luckily, it was our last stop for the day. My head was buzzing pleasantly. Then it kind of settled after I ate two large helpings of the freshest and most delicious lobster I've ever tasted. It was so much fun. I'm so glad you booked me on this trip. Love you son," she said, her voice breathless with excitement.

"Mom, I'm so glad to know you are enjoying yourself," grinned Arjun, finally at peace for the first time after she had fallen ill. Parth's company was obviously doing her a lot of good.

He asked to speak to the man himself. "Hello Parth, thank you."

"There he goes again with his 'vote of thanks'. Arjun, will you stop saying 'thank you' all the time? Do you really think I am doing *you* a favour?"

Arjun guffawed. "I know what you mean."

"And thank you, buddy, for keeping busy. Just now..."

"I know," said Arjun, continuing to laugh.

"Oh-kay! That was premeditated," said Parth, an answering grin in his voice.

"Yep! I definitely don't want to play gooseberry."

"Thank you for being such a wonderful son, Arjun."

Arjun said "bye" before switching off his cell, glad that his mother was recovering so well.

76

P arth was all packed as they were leaving the next day. He had had the most memorable stay in Greece, with Anjali for company. And how he managed to restrain himself through these ten days was the biggest wonder. He was in love for the first time in his life while he also found Anjali physically enticing. Keeping his hands off her hadn't been easy. Parth sighed. But he didn't want her to feel pressurised in any way. He wasn't renowned for his patience. It was a new trait he had acquired recently, it seemed.

He heard a soft knock on his door. He couldn't believe his eyes when he saw Anjali standing outside. "Come in," he said, taking her hand and pulling her inside. She was wearing a dressing gown which almost touched her feet. Though tired, she was obviously wide awake.

"Not able to sleep?" he asked, running his hand through her silky hair, unable to resist.

She shook her head, her eyes calling out to him. Was he reading her correctly?

"Anjali..." He pulled her into his arms. He kissed her luscious lips when she lifted her face to his. The kiss sent them up in flames as their tongues duelled in delicious exploration.

Parth moved towards the bed, continuing to hold her in his arms. He sat on the bed before pulling her down into his lap. He traced her features with his lips as Anjali purred in his arms. His teeth bit an earlobe gently as she groaned.

"Anjali, are you sure?" he asked, raising his head to look at her flushed face. She opened her passionate gaze to look up at him.

She placed her arms around his neck before pressing her lips to his ear. "Never more so in my life," she whispered.

Parth smiled into her hair as he pulled the knot on her dressing gown, whistling when he saw her wearing a red, transparent nightie which barely covered her thighs. "Sexy!" he said, kissing her again, lifting his hand to touch her breast.

He heard her moan loudly and took his hand away quickly. "Did I hurt you?" He had been quite gentle.

She shook her head, her eyes shut tightly. "No," she said, taking his hand and placing it back on her breast. "Please don't stop."

Parth traced his thumb over a taut nipple. She was obviously sensitive despite the thin material covering her. "Uncharted territory?" he asked tenderly.

She nodded, a lone tear escaping her closed eyelids.

"My poor sweetheart," said Parth, bending down to capture the nipple in his mouth.

They made love late into the night, as if there was no tomorrow. He was thrilled to discover her erogenous zones along with her as he delighted her, his hands and lips relentlessly caressing her body.

Only when he was sure that she was completely ready, he raised himself on his arms to ask, "May I?" He did his best to be gentle, though it wasn't easy with her thrashing about.

"Please Parth," she groaned.

77

njali's body felt worshipped, her previously untouched breasts feeling cherished with his lovemaking. She beseeched him to continue, trying to grab hold of something which seemed constantly out of her reach.

It felt as if it was her first time. And for all intents and purposes it was, as she had never been made *love* to before in her life.

Anjali felt her heart pound when he entered her slowly. She heard his grunt of satisfaction as he settled into the rhythm as old as time. She responded enthusiastically, clinging to his shoulders, her legs going around his waist. She felt herself floating up in the sky as he continued to love her. Soon, Anjali groaned long and loud when she felt stars exploding in front of her eyes even as she felt her first orgasm blast forth from within. Parth continued to pound inside her as she held him close, waiting for him to join her in the celebration. Incredibly, she reached a second climax along with him.

She refused to let go when he tried to move away. "Shh love, I'm going nowhere. I just don't want to crush you with my weight," he said as he settled close to her.

She snuggled into his chest, kissing his shoulder. "Parth!" she whispered, her voice cracking, "That was the most incredible experience of my life."

She felt Parth's smile against her forehead before he placed a hand under her chin to raise her face to his. "I know you're planning to leave your husband, Anjali. This might be too early. But... will you marry me? I will wait as long as you want. I promise not to rush you. But I want to spend the rest of my life with you."

Anjali traced a finger over his masculine lips. She felt so free with him, as if she could do anything and he would never reject her. That was the level of comfort she felt with this man whom she had met for the first time only a couple of months ago. Even after being married for two decades, she was on pins around Jayant. But did that mean she was ready to tie herself down with another man?

"Thank you, Parth for giving me the highest honour. Will you mind terribly if I don't give you my answer right now? I want to get away from Jayant first and explore life on my own. I know I am falling for you in a big way. But right now, I am scared of committing myself. Do you understand that?" *What if he told her to get lost? Well, in that case, he obviously wasn't the man for her.*

Parth didn't disappoint her as he gave a firm nod. "No worries love. We get married if and when you want to. Otherwise, I still plan to be a part of your life. If you continue to let me make love to you, I will consider that a bonus."

"And what if I want to make love to you? Will you let me?" Yes, Anjali had decided to stick to her bold, aggressive avatar. It was time she stopped leading a fake life.

Parth's laugh rented the air as he let her have her way with him, to Anjali's absolute delight.

Jayant was satisfied with his lot. It was barely forty-eight hours since Anjali had got back home and everything had been set in order. Well, she was still not talking to him unless you could count the monosyllabic answers she came up with. But the house ran on oiled wheels.

Better yet, Seema was happy and friendly, even ready to meet him privately most evenings. He was seriously considering buying her a small flat of her own right here in Hiranandani Gardens. That way, he wouldn't need to travel too far to spend time with her. Nor would she need to rush to Mulund to her miniscule flat a few times every week.

Rubbing his hands in glee, Jayant set to work on his latest project, nailing all the details in place. He truly was having the best of both worlds and must be the luckiest man on the planet.

He opened the front door of his apartment silently at 1.30 am and entered stealthily into his own home. It was a good thing Anjali slept in the room at the back of the apartment as it had become more convenient for his late-night jaunts.

What he hadn't expected was for his wife to be sitting in the hall, reading. Well, she would ignore him anyway, he thought, as he turned towards his bedroom.

"Jayant, please sit down here for a few minutes. I have something important to discuss with you."

He turned to glare at her. Couldn't she see that he was tired after a hard day's work? While she must have had a merry time. Okay, granted that she had gone back to work immediately after returning from her holiday. But she spent barely three hours at doing that research for Bhardwaj. And it wasn't as if it was a major responsibility she carried on her shoulders.

Frowning heavily, he said, "I'm sure it can wait till tomorrow morning. I am beat."

"No Jayant, it can't wait till tomorrow morning," she said firmly, much to his astonishment.

What's with the woman! He gritted his teeth as he threw his briefcase on a chair before taking an about turn and walking towards her. "I need coffee if you want to have a chat with me." His voice brooked no argument.

He sat down on the sofa and watched Anjali as she walked to the kitchen. His scowl deepened. There was something different about her, a... a new confidence in her stride. Her shoulders were straighter and her movements more fluid. He waited in silence as she brought two cups of coffee and placed the tray on a side table. There was a glow about her face which he hadn't noticed before. Shrewd businessman that he was, Jayant couldn't help but wonder what must have happened to bring about such a change in Anjali. Could holidaying abroad, that too alone, do it to a person?

Anjali sat on the opposite sofa, sipping her coffee.

Jayant finished his in a few gulps and said, "Go on, tell me what you have to. I have a full day tomorrow and would like to get some sleep before that."

"I want a divorce," stated Anjali, baldly.

"What? Have you taken leave of your senses?" shouted Jayant, shocked to the core of his being. His happiness of the morning went to pieces with that one stray sentence from her lips.

Anjali shook her head. "More like I have regained my senses after all this time." Her calm voice grated on his nerves.

He shouted at her for the next half an hour, sleep forgotten. "It's your identity as Mrs Mathur which gives you the prestige and entry into so many high society homes. You will be nothing once my name is removed from yours. You..."

Jayant didn't bother to check if she was listening to him. He went on and on until it finally struck him that his wife was not saying anything, not even the monosyllables which he had been hearing these last few months.

That was when he changed his tactics and began cajoling her. The words stuck in his throat. While he was used to being persuasive in his business tactics, he had always taken Anjali for granted. It never struck him before now to coax her into doing something for him. He had always shouted his orders and she listened. But this woman in front of him had changed. So, he decided to beguile her with honeyed words.

"I know you are upset that I didn't go with you to Greece. So what? We can surely go on another holiday. This time, I'll book the tickets myself. You choose where you want to go. Would you like to go to Las Vegas? Or maybe Johannesburg? I will take you wherever you want. And we can go next week, once the bookings are done. I will have all my appointments cancelled. Just think of the life you are living here Anjali. You are my queen, ruling over my home and heart. Don't do things in a rush and spoil our happy lives."

No answer. Had she gone to sleep on him? He glared at her balefully, knowing fully well that she was wide awake and not budging an inch.

Jayant finally played his trump card. "Think of Arjun. Our son will be heartbroken if he hears of us going separate. At least for his sake, we need to stay together." This should surely work as his wife thought the world of their son.

"He knows."

And Jayant started shouting again.

79

rjun held the phone to his ear while his father ranted on and on about his ungrateful mother. He waited silently for him to have his say, not interrupting him. Arjun could understand his father's grievances. His life would undergo a drastic change if his mother left him. But then change was the only constant in life. No one could escape that.

While he loved his father and admired him as a businessman, Arjun believed that his mother had got a raw deal in their marriage. Well, no one can do much about what had already happened. But there was still the rest of her life. She needed to find happiness. And he knew that Parth adored his mother.

"Are you listening to me Arjun?" asked Jayant in an angry voice.

"Yeah Dad, I am."

"Don't you have anything to say? Your mother says that you already know that she wants a divorce. And when the hell did she make the decision? How long have you known about it? You never thought of sharing that bit of news with your old Dad," he accused.

"Dad, listen. Please calm down. Would you have liked it if I had told you that? It's best that Mom spoke to you directly about it. And..."

"She has turned you also against me. I am really hurt. My whole family is against me. What am I working so hard for? This huge business that has been eating into my heart while I have been working such long hours, all for what? It's for the two of you, my only family. And both of you don't care about me."

Arjun grinned at his father's childish tantrums. He knew that Jayant loved his business and thrived on it. And his heart was strong too. The yearly medical tests which he underwent were proof of that.

"Dad, please chill. You *know* I love you. And so does Mom, in her own way." Well, that was an exaggeration, but the situation called for it.

"Don't you dare tell me that your mother loves me! She doesn't give a damn what happens to me. Otherwise, she won't demand for a divorce. Twenty years of my life I have given to her. And this is how she repays me," he growled.

Arjun would have laughed if it wasn't so sad. It was truly the other way around. His mother had given away twenty years of her life and what did she have in return? A lot of wealth which she didn't really need. But his father would never understand that.

"Dad, I'm sorry. I know you are terribly upset. But I think you should let go of Mom. Allow her to live her life the way she wants to. I know it will take some time, but I'm sure you will be fine," he said softly.

"If she thinks she's going to make me pay her a hefty alimony, she's thoroughly mistaken. Let her fend for herself. I don't give a damn. I am ready to take responsibility for my wife. But once she divorces me, she can go to hell."

Arjun smiled to himself, a mite sadly. No, his father would never understand his mother, not in the next million years.

80

Anjali sat in front of Jayant as he read her yet another lecture. But it was a bit different this time. He had obviously heard some new gossip.

"What's this I hear about you and Parth? Is it true he went to Greece with you?" he thundered.

"Yes," nodded Anjali.

"What? How dare you? No wonder you were only too happy when I cancelled my trip. So, this is what has been happening behind my back. And I have trusted you, always. I never in my wildest dreams would have imagined that you will betray me like this. I have been nurturing a snake all these years..."

"That's unfair Jayant," said Anjali, her voice soft, in direct contrast to his shouting. "I've never looked at another man, let alone befriended one; despite being aware of your multiple love affairs since ages. But things changed from the moment you flaunted your mistress so openly at the party that day. You are fully aware that I went into depression. If not for Arjun's intervention and later on, getting to know Parth, chances were high that I would have never recovered.

And no thanks to you! I know you don't give a damn about me. What I can't understand is why I put up with it for twenty years. I..."

"Oh, you put up with me for twenty years, did you? Was it probably the luxurious life which came along with me?" Jayant was at his sarcastic best.

Anjali shrugged. "I suppose it must be that. Otherwise, what other motivation was there? It was definitely neither the love nor the sex which kept me at your side." She gave back as good as she got.

Jayant snarled; his fists clenched. He spouted abuse on her head. She could see that his ego was unable to accept her insults. Nothing like truth to kick one's butt!

Anjali refused to let his words hurt her. Jayant meant nothing to her. Just a while longer and she would be free of him forever.

But Providence had other plans it seemed.

After shouting for the better part of fifteen minutes with no reaction from his wife, Jayant paused and said, "Okay, have it your way. I'll give you a divorce, and alimony; though nothing in the standards you are used to. That honour can be yours only till you remain my wife. I need something in exchange."

Anjali looked at him and asked, "What?"

"You don't move out of here for the next six months. We..."

"Don't be crazy Jayant. That will only delay our divorce. What's the sense?" she asked, panicking. It had been difficult to arrive at the decision. But once she had got there, she was keen to be free to do her own thing.

"No, no, listen to me first. We'll apply for divorce, this week. But you continue to stay here for some time. I don't want to lose face with anyone. Let me plan this out and we will go our separate ways without any fanfare. Do you get me?" he asked.

Anjali looked into his eyes searchingly. What was he planning? Will he stick to his word? Could she trust him?

But then what choice did she have? After twenty years, six months did seem like a short span.

"Okay!" she sighed, giving him a reluctant nod.

Jayant gave a sigh of relief when Anjali agreed for the six-month wait. He had been thinking hard since the night she had asked him for a divorce.

They had grown far apart and she wasn't the wife he needed any more. He should probably get himself a younger woman who had better health and was more amiable. But all that will come later.

Just now, he needed time to get Seema out of the picture. That woman had begun to cling. If she got wind that he was getting divorced, she will definitely want him to tie the knot with her. As she had been a virgin before they got together, chances were high that she would become demanding. It had been fun bedding Seema, but Jayant didn't want to get together permanently with his executive assistant, of all women. She wasn't even from a high-class background.

When he married Anjali, Jayant had been on the first rung of the success ladder. Today, he was the uncrowned king of the business world. He will have to choose his life partner with care. Yes, he would do it.

And as for Anjali getting close to Parth, he didn't really care. She was ice cold in bed. The poor man didn't know what he was letting himself for. What she had going for her were barely a few things—she was a great hostess and she kept his home running smoothly. Beyond that, she was useless. And now her health was also not that great. Jayant should thank his lucky stars that she had chosen to leave him of her own accord.

He needed some time to set up the exact front to portray to the world. All his relatives, friends and business associates need to be convinced that he was the one who was divorcing Anjali, and not the other way around.

Of course, he could do it.

82

arth knew of Anjali's promise to stay back with her husband while the divorce was being processed. He didn't have an opinion about it as long as she didn't have a problem with it. Breaking off a tie which was twenty years old couldn't be easy. Maybe, it was for the best that they were taking it slow.

Things hadn't changed as Anjali continued to work for him. And they spent some of the afternoons in bed, the sex mind blowing. He so enjoyed the aggressive woman in his bed. He grinned at his laptop as he attempted to write, though the scene from this afternoon kept interposing.

He had been asleep when she let herself into his apartment. His breathing changed when he sensed her presence, though he kept his eyes closed, just to see what she did. Parth had been amazed with her innovations. Keeping his lips straight was a task as he felt a strong urge to smile.

He felt her breath in his ear as she said, "I know you are awake. But tell me if you want coffee or me?"

Parth opened one eye in a half slit, giving in to the urge to grin. "Hmm... let me think. I..."

"Maybe you'd prefer to have the decision taken out of your hands? It must be difficult, working your brain so hard immediately on waking up," said her amused voice as she placed her lips on his.

He lay back on his bed, giving in to her exploration. Her tongue traced the shape of his mouth, the upper lip first and then the lower one. When she sought entry into his mouth, he let her in, groaning with need.

"Anjali."

Her fingers traced his features, before holding her hands to his cheeks, caressing her palms against his stubble. "I love your five o'clock shadow against my body. Want to explore?" she enticed.

He had been busy pulling off her sari. He pressed his lips to her décolletage, gently rubbing his cheeks against her.

"Parth!" she groaned, removing the rest of her clothes in a hurry. As he gently suckled the tip of one breast, she took his hand and placed it on the other. He felt her hands in his hair before she went on to stroke his shoulders, holding him close, her limbs entwined with his.

She purred in delight as she felt the friction of his face down the length her soft body. When she was fully aroused and wet with need, he went on his back and pulled her on top of him.

She held his face in her hands and looked into his eyes. "Show me how to please you, Parth. I don't know much," she said innocently.

"You've been doing pretty well over the last few weeks for someone who doesn't know much," he teased, taking her hand and placing it against his manhood.

She caressed him lovingly, her face buried in his chest. She gently touched a tongue to a flat male nipple. "Does it excite you as much as it does me when you do that?" she asked, biting him gently.

Parth almost jumped off the bed as if electrified. Grinning, she continued to nibble on him, even as her hand pleasured him below.

"Whoa! You are turning out to be dynamite in bed," he grinned, lifting her hips and entering her in one stroke.

New to the position, Anjali's eyes went wide in pleased surprise. "Parth!" she gasped. "I'm so loving it."

And just when things were falling in place for her, Jayant was murdered.

When Radha came wailing out of his bedroom, Anjali had been lighting the lamp in the *pooja* room. She rushed out even as Sita ran out of the kitchen.

"*Saab... saab,*" howled Radha, "*maine kuch nahi kiya.*"

Anjali rushed into Jayant's bedroom, the room where she hadn't stepped into in the last six months. She trembled when she saw the state Jayant was in. Rushing to him, she checked his pulse to find it missing. Her face completely draining of colour even as tears ran down her cheeks, she dialled Parth from her mobile.

He reached the flat within five minutes. Anjali fell into his arms, sobbing. "I never wished it on him, Parth. Why? Why did this have to happen? Who would hate him so much to shoot him in cold blood? Jayant's only fault was that he loved himself and none else. But he didn't deserve to die like this."

Parth held her without uttering a word as Anjali cried long and hard. "Poor Jayant. He has always worked so hard. Okay, he lived his life the way he chose and I didn't agree with it. But he was only forty-seven," she whispered in a broken voice. "Why? My son needs his father, Parth. He is so young, still at college. This can't happen to him. Arjun will go to pieces." Her voice choked.

She was also angry that it had happened on her watch. "I feel so responsible with Arjun so far away. And I was going to leave him in a few months. Why now?"

It took Parth a while to calm her down, his hand stroking her back rhythmically. "Don't blame yourself, my love. I am terribly sorry that he died this way. But you can't hold yourself responsible."

Anjali looked at him with tear drenched eyes. "Oh Parth! Poor Arjun, poor Jayant. Oh, what a bloody thing to happen!"

Her tears soon reduced to hiccups as she sipped the cup of tea pressed into her hands by Sita, at Parth's instigation. "What should I do now?" she asked him pathetically.

"You wash your face first and let's call Arjun. He needs to be told. I'll handle the rest of the things. Do you have your doctor's phone number saved somewhere?"

Anjali nodded, relieved that someone was there to shoulder her burden. She took deep breaths, doing her best to calm down as Parth handled everything. He even called the police and Jayant's relatives.

84

Samrat began his investigation meticulously, as always. He interviewed Anjali Mathur, Arjun Mathur and Parth Bhardwaj first. Later, he took the addresses and phone numbers of the victim's sisters and parents. He visited each family and asked them a number of questions.

He kept his opinion to himself when Rana Sahni insisted that Anjali and Parth were the murderers. He recorded every bit of conversation he held with each person.

The next day, he visited Jayant Mathur's friends who lived in the colony. Once he was done, on Day Three he went to Mathur's office. The company continued to run smoothly despite the owner's death. Yes, the rumour mill was churning a lot of gossip but then it was Samrat's job to separate the wheat from the chaff.

He took time and spoke to each and every one of the staff members. All had only good things to say about Jayant Mathur. He couldn't make out if they meant it or whether they were paying lip service.

Samrat got the list of names of people who were absent and went back the next day. It took him three days to talk to everyone, except for Jayant Mathur's executive assistant. She was on long leave for health reasons, he was told.

He spoke to the office attendant Ronak. "From when has Seema madam been absent?" He placed a hand on the man's shoulder, leading him to the cafeteria. He bought him a cup of tea. It was usually the employees in the lowest rung who got ignored. But Samrat knew from experience that these were the ones who were the gold mines of information.

"*Pata nahi saab*. It has been a long time," said Ronak. "*Ek minute*! I remember now. Arjun sir called the office two days after Jayant sir died. He wanted to talk to Seema madam. But madam had already gone on leave. I went and checked the dates. She hasn't been coming from the morning since Jayant sir's death." He looked this way and that before moving closer to Samrat. "*Woh dhonon ke beech mein kuch kuch chal raha tha*," he whispered.

"Between who two?" asked Samrat, keen that the man should give him exact names.

"Jayant sir *aur* Seema madam *ke beech mein*," replied Ronak.

"What was happening between them? Do explain clearly Ronak. This could be important," said Samrat.

Ronak looked around again and said, "The two of them were having an affair."

That was news to him. Wasn't Anjali Mathur aware of it? No one had mentioned it to Samrat. "Since when?" he asked.

"More than a year."

"How do you know? Have you seen them together?"

Ronak giggled. "Everyone in the office knows, sir. Seema madam used to leave exactly two minutes after Jayant sir left, every day. And," his voice turned even lower. "I believe they went to the service apartment in Powai. That flat belongs to the office."

Samrat looked at the man sternly. "How do you know about that? Don't tell me lies Ronak. How can you say they went to the other flat, sitting here in the office? You should not gossip like this. You might lose your job if Arjun Mathur gets to know."

Ronak shook his head vigorously. "The truth is that I have never seen them there. But the same team of cleaners work in both places. The staff keeps rotating. They have seen things and everyone talks."

Samrat nodded. "Do you remember who spoke to you about this? The exact person? Arrange for me to talk to this person," he insisted.

Ronak nodded. "You can talk now itself, sir. Champa has come to the office today."

Late at night, Samrat sat in Parth's penthouse, listening to all the tapes he had recorded. He concluded that the missing piece was Seema Dodhia. Unless he spoke to her, the investigation could go no further.

85

rjun took the call on the second ring. It was the private detective. "Hello Samrat, tell me."

"Arjun, I've just sent you an SMS. I need you to come to this address in Mulund immediately. It would be even better if you can bring the police with you. I think I have found your father's murderer."

Arjun paled, turning desperate eyes to Parth who came to his side immediately, realising that something was afoot. "Who is it, Samrat? Anyone we know?" His voice shook as adrenaline rushed through him.

"It's Ms Seema Dodhia, your father's executive assistant."

Arjun didn't know what else he said before disconnecting the phone. He turned to Parth and buried his face against the older man's shoulder and cried. His hands inadvertently tugged at Parth's shirt; his anguish unbearable.

What had his father ever done to deserve this from the woman? Arjun had been vaguely aware of his father's extra-marital affairs. There had been talk of some woman at his office. But why should that lead to him being murdered?

He pulled himself together and straightened. "Parth, it's Dad's assistant Seema who's the culprit, says Samrat. He wants me to go to her place with the police. I..."

"I'll call Inspector Phadke and inform him. You forward me the address by Whatsapp. I'll also go with you."

When Arjun opened his mouth to thank him, Parth said, "No Arjun. Don't you dare thank me again," hugging the younger man.

Arjun sighed, nodding. Parth was truly a Godsend. Not just for his mother but for him as well.

"And Arjun, let's not say anything to Anjali right now."

Arjun nodded, even as Parth called Inspector Phadke.

She was fed up of hiding in her flat, worrying when the police would find her. Find her they will. But Seema didn't have the guts to surrender herself.

Her only defence was that she never meant to kill him. But who would accept that? Tears coursed down her cheeks. She hadn't stopped crying since that fateful night.

One minute he had been there full of life and the next he was no more, his eyes looking at the ceiling lifelessly.

She felt horrified every time she recalled the incident, which was in every waking moment. Which was again, twenty-four hours a day. She was unable to sleep, unable to eat, unable to do anything. Grief and guilt ate into her, making her want to die. She had sent a message to the office, pleading sickness. She didn't care if she had a job to go to. What did anything matter?

Today, it had been a relief when the private detective knocked on her door. The moment she saw him, she knew that her secret was out. Relief had been the strongest emotion.

She told him everything—her relationship with Jayant and what had happened that night. Finally, she sagged against her sofa, shutting her eyes as sleep claimed her with its unexpected suddenness.

87

Samrat was amazed at human nature. This woman professed to have loved Jayant Mathur, while she had also been instrumental to his death. Whether she was the murderer, it was for the police and maybe Jayant's family to decide.

But he was satisfied with a job well done. While the enquiries had been tedious—typical of a private eye's life—in the end the investigation had been quite simple. He had just needed to put the jigsaw together and find the missing piece.

The moment he saw Seema Dodhia on the other side of the door, he knew she had been responsible for Jayant Mathur's death. She was haggard to put it mildly. Her clothes hung loosely on her frame as if she had lost a lot of weight recently. Her face was streaked with tears while her eyes and nose were swollen and red.

More than anything, he was startled to see the relief in her eyes when he announced himself. She had let him into her tiny flat, sat him down and offered him water.

"Go on, ask me your questions. I will tell you only the truth and nothing but the truth," she said, steadying her trembling voice.

Samrat listened to her for the next half an hour, without interrupting her even once and of course, recording her confession.

In the end, he wasn't too surprised when she put her head back on the sofa and went to sleep. He was sure the woman hadn't slept a wink since Jayant's death.

That was when he called Arjun and requested him to come over with the police.

Seema's confession...

Seema was thrilled to bits when she found out she was pregnant. She had used a pregnancy kit to check when her periods were delayed by more than ten days and the test had showed positive. She fixed an appointment with her gynaecologist and went to meet her the same day.

Dr Desai conducted a few tests before saying, "Congratulations Ms Dodhia, you are approximately six weeks pregnant. You appear to be in excellent health. Since you are not on any medication, I will prescribe you some vitamins and iron. You take them regularly. Stay off any kind of alcohol, not even wine or beer," she warned, smiling at the mother-to-be.

Seema went red in the face, her excitement palpable. She nodded vigorously. "Is there anything else I should or should not do, Dr Desai?"

"Lead as normal a life as possible. Just be careful when travelling on bad roads. It would be ideal if you can avoid going around in auto-rickshaws. Otherwise, you can eat all kinds of food. Drink a lot of water to avert morning sickness. It would be best if you can avoid eating a heavy dinner late at night. Try to have your last meal by eight. You can maybe have a glass of warm milk and fresh fruits later. Go for a walk for at least half an hour every day. You can see me again four weeks from now," said Dr Desai.

Seema nodded once again, making a mental note of all the points. After paying her bill and fixing her next appointment with the receptionist, she left the clinic, floating on air. She was sure that Jayant would be glad to hear that he was to become a father again.

Okay, maybe, just maybe, he might not want to advertise the fact; what with his reputation at stake. But he would surely be happy with the news. Seema straightened her shoulders. She'll make sure he was.

Seema went along with Jayant for their regular tryst the next evening. It hadn't been easy, keeping the news to herself for more than twenty-four hours. She was simply dying to share it with him.

She could see he was surprised when she insisted on having fruit juice instead of her usual drink. But he didn't ask her anything as she had hoped he would. Well, it looked like she would have to tell him directly.

"Jayant, I've something special to share with you," she said, her voice choking with happiness. "You and I..."

"Can it wait? I have some heavy thinking to do. I'd prefer if you stopped chattering."

Seema's face fell, not that he noticed. She waited quietly as he downed a few drinks, brooding.

"Can we talk now?" she asked, unable to contain herself. It had been an hour after all. Without waiting for his reply, Seema blurted out, "Jayant, I'm pregnant with your baby. Isn't that simply awesome?"

When his mouth fell wide open, she presumed it was in awe.

89

Jayant spluttered before he swallowed his drink in a hurry, his mouth falling open wide in shock. He had just taken a huge swallow of scotch when Seema gave her news. What the hell! How could this happen?

He glared at Seema's happy face. Damn the woman! Didn't she have better sense then to become pregnant? Over and above that, she was sounding so damn excited about it. What was there to feel happy about? Jayant saw his life falling apart right in front of him.

"How the hell did that happen?" he barked, not too bothered when the smile vanished from her face.

"What do you mean? The usual way, of course. How else do you think it could have happened?" she asked, getting angry.

"You fool! I'm not asking you that and you very well know it. How could you have got pregnant? I made sure that we used protection each time. I..."

"What are you suggesting? That the baby is not yours? How dare you?"

Jayant realised that he was making the situation worse than it already was. The last time Seema went into a sulk, he had borne the brunt of it. Right now, he wasn't in a state to manage two angry women. The one at home was more than enough.

He got up from his sofa to sit on the arm of hers. Putting his hand on her shoulder, he squeezed it gently. "You've got me wrong. Let me congratulate you first." He pressed his lips to her cheek, his mind working furiously. "It's just that I'm taking a while to digest this bit of news. I'm forty-seven. I didn't know I had it in me," he smiled sheepishly even as he fumed inside.

Seema blushed prettily, her temper vanishing. "I was surprised too. I'm not that young either," she whispered.

"We'll need to find you a good doctor. Let me see…"

"I found a gynaec, she comes highly recommended by a friend who has four kids. I went to see Dr Desai yesterday. I had been waiting for the right time to tell you," she said, enthusiastic once again.

Jayant got up to walk to the window. He needed to put some distance between them if he had to stop himself from strangling her. No, he needed her to visit some other doctor. And he knew exactly who it was.

He turned around and spoke to Seema, his voice brooking no argument. "You realise that you are pregnant with the Mathur heir? Okay, a second heir, but mine nonetheless. I don't want you to go to just any damn doctor. I will call a gynaecologist I know and highly recommend. I'll even fix an appointment for you. You change over to him."

He gave a grunt of satisfaction when Seema nodded her head slowly, her smile not quite reaching her eyes.

Seema was surprised when Dr Deshmukh insisted on admitting her in his private nursing home. Only the day before yesterday, Dr Desai had told her that she was in perfect health and her baby was doing fine. But this doctor, highly recommended by Jayant, insisted that she needed to stay back for observation over the next twenty-four hours.

Dr Deshmukh was much older and more experienced. And he was also obviously close to Jayant. Seema didn't see the sense in arguing with him and admitted herself into the nursing home. She called Jayant to inform him of the situation.

"Hello Jayant, Dr Deshmukh wants me to admit myself here for a day. I..."

"If the good doctor is saying so, then that's what you must do, Seema. There's no need to disturb me. I have already spoken to him and you will be taken complete care of. Just do what he tells you."

Seema wasn't happy with that. But then, this was her first baby. She didn't want to go against Jayant. She would need his support at every step. "Okay," she said, disconnecting the call.

A nurse came into the hospital room which resembled one in a five-star hotel. Smiling at Seema, she gave her a change of clothes. "Please change into this ma'am. The doctor will be with you soon."

Sometime later, Dr Deshmukh came in. "Hello Ms Dodhia. I will give you an injection to keep you calm. You sleep well tonight and tomorrow we will do a battery of tests on an empty stomach."

Seema stared at him. "I am calm doctor. I don't think I need an injection. I..."

"No, my dear. You are in a new place and you might not be able to sleep. Being well rested is extremely important," he insisted before administering the injection.

Seema felt her eyes closing within a few minutes, much to her shock. Had he just given her a sleeping draught? But she should not be taking strong medicines, not with a small life growing within her. Only she was fast sleep before she could find an answer to her question.

J ayant was startled when a figure separated itself from the shadows outside his flat. "Oh, it's you Seema," he smiled, or tried to, when he noticed her red face. Her eyes appeared dead while the tears had dried on her cheeks.

Thinking on his feet, he opened the door to his flat, and checked the area for Anjali. When he saw that she was not there in the hallway, he pulled Seema roughly into his bedroom.

"What are you doing here at this time of the night?" he snarled, shutting the door firmly. His room was soundproofed to help him sleep better as even the smallest of noises tended to wake him up. "Are you aware that it's past one am? What if Anjali had seen you?"

He refused to meet Seema's eyes when she glared at him, a sudden fire in her gaze. "Why did you kill my baby?"

"Don't be silly, Seema. How can you ask me such a question? It was my baby too or had I got that wrong?" he asked, trying to turn the tables on her.

Tears coursed down Seema's face. "You may have been the biological father, but the baby was never yours. How could you do this Jayant? If only you had told me once that you didn't want the child, I'd have gone away and left you in peace."

Jayant's eyes widened in shock! Maybe he should have done just that. Had he been stupid in getting her aborted? The trouble he had gone to swear Dr Deshmukh into secrecy and the exorbitant amount he had paid for it—had everything been a waste? He wanted to kick at something.

"Are you sure?" he asked. "I'm a source of income for the people around me. You would have only blackmailed me," he said. His respectable image in society was very important to him and he didn't want anyone talking badly of him. That was his only fear. Abortion had seemed like the ideal solution. Even now, he still believed it had been for the best. If the child had lived, what if someone recognised the baby as his? It had carried his genes.

Seema cried piteously. "How dare you, Jayant? Just to maintain your prestige, how could you kill such a tiny being? So helpless too? Did you even think of me?" she grabbed hold of his coat jacket and shook him, or tried to. Jayant didn't budge.

"Calm down, Seema," he ordered, pulling her hands off his jacket. "Do something," he said, indicating a small bar and fridge in one corner of the room. "Mix us some drinks. I need to get out of these formals." He walked into the adjoining bathroom, confident of her obedience.

To his surprise, when he came out, Jayant found Seema standing exactly where he had left her. He patted the bed and said, "Okay, you sit down and get comfortable. I will get our drinks."

"No," she screamed. "You have to give me an answer. How dare you kill my baby? The least you could have done was ask me." He noticed that her eyes were wild, red with temper.

"Listen, what's done is done. We can't turn back the clock. You tell me what you want me to do now. I..."

Seema shook her head. "It's your money and prestige which are talking, not the human being in you. You killed my baby so that you won't be shamed in society. Just watch me. I'm going to drag your name through mud." Saying this, she turned towards the door as if to leave.

Jayant removed his gun from the bedside drawer. That was something he'd never tolerate, his name tarnished. "I warn you Seema. Just forget that you got pregnant. Better yet, forget that you ever met me. If you are amiable, I'll ensure that you are financially well off and get a reference to take to your next job. If you threaten me..." he shook the gun at her, his message obvious.

In a few strides, Seema was standing in front of him. "Go on, shoot me and end this torture," she screamed at him.

Jayant didn't quite know how to handle the situation. Maybe he should cajole her. He placed the gun above the drawer and sat down on the bed, pulling her beside him.

"Let's not fight Seema. I'm tired of everything. What do you want me to say? That I'm sorry? Okay, I am sorry that I got the abortion done. Alright? Let's forget everything and begin a new life."

He lay down on the bed and tried to pull her into his arms. He was truly very tired after a long day and the emotional drama.

The next second, the gun was in Seema's hand as she sat on his stomach, aiming it against his chest.

"How does it feel being at the receiving end of this?" she asked, grinning madly.

Jayant was shocked. He put his hands up in surrender saying, "Be careful Seema. The safety lock is off. The pistol will go off. Keep it away." His voice was soft and pleading. He was scared of talking loudly just in case he spooked her.

Seema laughed loudly; her brain obviously scrambled. "Do you good Mr Businessman. It will sure do you good to worry. You didn't think twice before snuffing my baby's life. Why should I not do the same to you?" she challenged, the gun swinging this way and that as her hand trembled.

"Seema, listen to me. Why don't we talk about this?" Jayant tried to get up, but she pressed her left hand on his chest, pushing him down. He stopped as he didn't want her to shoot him, though he was confident that he could dissuade her from doing it. She was not a killer. She was just reacting to the situation. It had really been stupid on his part to take the gun out in the first place. "Seema," he called again, his voice appealing.

But she was crying, tears pouring down her face. Though her index finger stayed on the trigger, she was in no state to shoot the weapon. Relieved, Jayant lifted his hand to remove the pistol from hers and a shot rang out, reverberating in the bedroom.

His shocked eyes met hers as pain splintered his chest and the last thing he saw was her mouth open in a scream before he stopped breathing.

92

"Iwas shocked, to put it mildly, screaming my head off. But within a few seconds, my brain kicked in. It's simply mind-boggling how the brain comes to one's rescue in an emergency. Here I was, having committed the most gruesome act of my life—I truly don't know which one of us pressed the trigger, but I was holding the gun."

"Worse yet, he was dead and I was still alive. I got off him, removed a small towel from my handbag and wiped the gun clean, dropping it on the carpet beside the bed. Then I walked to the locked door and listened for a minute. There was absolute silence. Was no one else home? I opened the door, careful enough to cover my hand with the same towel. I was clear about not leaving any fingerprints. When I peeped outside, there was no one there. Either there was nobody at home or they were stone deaf. How could someone not have heard the gunshot and my scream?"

"It was quite simple to walk out of the front door after that. I went down the staircase to the sixth floor. Yes, reading Agatha Christie and Perry Mason novels came in very helpful. The liftman obviously must have presumed that I was visiting someone on that floor and not the tenth floor where Jayant lived. It was too simple to walk out of the building, reach the main road, take a rickshaw and go home."

"But what I had not expected was that I wouldn't be able to live with myself, not after the way Jayant died that night."

Arjun heard the dry sobs just before Samrat switched off the recorder. His face was pale as he sat next to Parth, gripping his hand tightly. Was it his father's own fault that he had died? Tears streamed down Arjun's face.

What a pathetic way to die! His father! The man whom he had hero worshipped! The one he had admired throughout his life. Jayant had been so successful with his business, having started it from scratch and building it up to a turnover of a couple of billions per year. His meteoric rise was like a fairy tale and Arjun had so loved to hear about it again and again.

But right now, his heart broke when he got to know about the way his father's life had been snuffed out, just like that.

He turned to look at the sleeping woman. Seema was still seated on the floor, her head leaning against the sofa, her eyes shut in deep sleep.

For a moment, Arjun felt such a powerful sense of hatred towards her. It roiled within him like poison as he glared at her sleeping figure, his eyes red as they burned with loathing. It was she who was responsible for his father's death.

Arjun got up to walk towards the window, staring unseeingly out at the road, his body shuddering as he tried to control his grief, his hands clenched into tight fists.

Hatred was not the answer. It was corrosive, hurting both the giver and the receiver. Isn't that what his mother had taught him throughout his life? What was the use of hating Seema? Would that bring his father back to life? Or would it absolve Jayant of all his mistakes? That his father had made a number of mistakes was something Arjun couldn't deny.

Taking deep breaths, he forced himself to calm down before turning to look at Parth who was seated next to Samrat, not having uttered a word.

Parth really knew when to keep his silence, thought Arjun, walking towards the other man, accepting his hug when he got up to offer his support.

Arjun sighed. "It's all so ugly. I never thought my father would stoop this low," he said softly, only for Parth's ears.

Parth patted Arjun on his shoulder, shaking his head slowly. "Don't beat yourself, Arjun. In all my years, the one thing I have realised is that nobody is perfect. Your father was only human. He had both his pluses and minuses, just like everyone else."

Arjun looked into the intelligent gaze of the man who had become such a close friend and confidante over the past months, trying to smile but failing. "What to do now? I..." he lifted a shoulder in a half-shrug, "I don't know what to do. We don't even know who pulled the trigger, if it was my Dad or his...

his…" he didn't complete the sentence, pointing his chin in Seema's direction. "You know what I mean." He sighed; his eyes heavy with pain.

He felt torn. Though he found it difficult to swallow, the truth was that Seema had been wronged too. She had lost her baby, all because an abortion had been forced on her and that too by his father.

And then there was her guilt as she wasn't sure if it was she who had pulled the trigger the other night.

Wasn't living with her guilt a big enough punishment? He was torn between feeling sorry for his dead father and for the living Seema. Another deep sigh shuddered from the depths of Arjun's being.

He looked first at Parth and then at Inspector Phadke. The latter said, "This could probably be the simplest as well as the most difficult case, Mr Mathur. Presuming Ms Seema Dodhia is telling us the truth, hiding away in her flat after removing her fingerprints from the murder weapon speaks of guilt. She could have surrendered herself to the police immediately. The law is quite strict in these matters."

"But isn't there something called compassion?" The words were torn out of Arjun, his sense of righteousness coming to the fore. "This woman is grieving two deaths, not one. There must be some way that she's not made to suffer more."

Parth gave Arjun a soft smile, nodding his head slowly. "I'm sure your mother will be extremely proud of you, Arjun. As will your father as he watches you from above. *Chalo*, let's see what can be done. I am sure the lawyer will be able to help us."

Seema Dodhia locked up her tiny flat and left with Phadke and the police woman who had come along while the trio of Arjun, Parth and Samrat headed for home.

Arjun reached home and hugged his anxious mother. "Mom," he sighed. "It was all Dad's fault. He was responsible for his own death." His voice broke, even as his father's image splintered in his mind. How much he had respected him! Arjun struggled valiantly to hold back his tears of anger. Not for a minute did he believe that Seema may have lied. There was enough evidence floating around to corroborate her. And it would probably be child's play for Samrat to acquire the information regarding the abortion. Well, all that was for the court to deal with. He and Parth had work to do, speak to the lawyer and find out how best to help Seema.

93

I n the end, Seema was sentenced to three years of imprisonment. She was aware and grateful that Arjun and Parth had tried their best, but they couldn't help her beyond that.

They went to meet her one last time before she was taken away to jail. Tears in her eyes, Seema said, "Thank you so much Arjun. If it was not for you, I would probably have been given life imprisonment."

Arjun nodded his head. "You take care, Seema," he said, before turning to go.

"*Kaash*! If only your father had one hundredth of your caring nature! If he had been a good person, our lives would have been so much better." Seema's voice was regretful.

Arjun turned around in a flash, his brown eyes blazing with temper. "How dare you?" he snarled; his voice low. "How dare you besmirch my father's name? *Kaash* indeed! *If*', he stressed, "if my father had been anything like me, he wouldn't have had an affair with you in the first place. And remember Seema, it takes two. You knew very well that he was married. But that didn't stop you from sleeping with him. And you have the gall to say that your life would have been better if he had been more like me? If he had been anything like me, he would have stayed loyal to his wife. And you would have remained his assistant and nothing more. Think of my mother. She's the one who's the victim in all this. Don't you dare shift the blame wholly to my father's shoulders!"

Saying that, he did an about turn and walked out, not bothering to wait for her reaction.

She watched him go, envious of Anjali. Arjun was fiercely loyal to his mother and Seema could see how supportive Parth was towards her. There was romance there for sure. Anjali was truly blessed! Seema's lips drooped. Some people were just born lucky.

EPILOGUE

njali was amazed that eight months were already gone after Jayant's death. All credit due to him, Parth never asked to make love to her even once during that time, though he had been a rock-solid support throughout—to both Arjun and her. Her son had missed one whole semester, while the court case was going on. Now he was back at Kingston, working hard. They were in touch often as time healed their wounds.

While she continued to help Parth with his research, Anjali had come into her own. She discovered that she had a flair for writing children's fiction.

Her first book had been accepted for publishing and an artist was getting the pictures ready for the same. Her target audience was age five to eight. and she was pretty excited about the project. She was so glad that Parth was there for her with an inspiring word here and an encouraging hug there, but only if she asked for it.

Anjali stroked the tiny head of Sam, her four-month-old kitten. Sam was grey with a white belly and paws. Parth had picked up the little stray which had been running around in the garden near his home, especially for her.

Yes, he is considerate that way, my Parth, thought Anjali, a soft smile spreading on her face. She was sure now that she belonged to him and planned to marry him if he would still have her.

She called him. "Hi Parth, are you busy? I was thinking of coming over."

"Never too busy for you, my sweetheart. Come along," he invited.

Anjali was dressed at her sexiest best in a sleeveless shift which stopped a few inches above her knees, the aquamarine shade flattering her golden complexion. She had a broad grin on her face when she walked into his penthouse, directly into his arms.

"Parth," she whispered in his ear, going on tiptoe and pressing her lips to his cheek. "I love you."

Parth crushed her in his arms, kissing her deeply, one hand holding her head, while the other caressed the back of a silken thigh. It was a long time before they came up for air.

Anjali's face was red as Parth drew a gentle finger down her neck, tracing the neckline of her dress. "It's been so long, sweetheart. I have missed making love to you," he whispered in her ear, a question in his voice.

"So have I, Parth. It's been too damn long. Will you please make love to me?" she asked.

She was startled when he lifted her up in his arms, her arms going around his neck in a hurry. "Oh my God! Parth, you're a caveman," she choked over a giggle which rose up her throat.

"A desperate caveman," he growled, placing her on the bed before joining her. Anjali lost her voice as his hands and lips were everywhere. Her dress came off, immediately followed by her bra and panties. The gentle Parth who had loved her all those other times was nowhere in sight. She watched him as he pulled off his t-shirt and belt. Getting off the bed, Anjali helped him remove his shorts and boxers quickly. It was not just he who was in a rush.

Their breath came in gasps as they devoured each other, not bothering to waste time on foreplay. Parth groaned as he entered her in one stroke, straining to make her his. They found their rhythm as they rose as one to reach up to the skies. "Parth," whimpered Anjali as she felt stars explode behind her closed eyelids.

They were soaked in sweat as Parth fell against her, taking deep breaths to calm his pounding heart. "I hope I didn't hurt you, sweetheart," he said, his forehead pressed to hers. His face was split wide in a grin.

Anjali shook her head, her smile as broad as his, her arms clinging to him. "Never, my Parth."

"Hey, what's this?" he asked, looking at the tattoo above her left breast. He traced the pattern with his forefinger, a look of wonder on his face. "It's..."

"Your autograph," she smiled shyly.

"You've inked my initials..."

"...close to my heart," she said in a whisper as he bent down to press his lips to the intertwined P and B. She wound her hands in his hair, holding him close as he traced the pattern with his tongue.

"Did it hurt badly?" he asked, looking up into her shining eyes.

Anjali shook her head, "Not at all." It was a whim and she had loved it. It was obvious Parth was dazed by what she had done.

"I'll have a shower." She got off the bed to follow action to words.

"Let's have one together," he got up too.

Anjali held his hand tightly, her heart thumping in excitement. Now this would be another new experience.

He led her to the adjoining bathroom, directly into the shower cubicle. He drove her crazy with his caresses while the warm shower added to the steam. His lips explored her mouth thoroughly, even as their tongues danced a tango. Anjali clung to his broad shoulders, rising on tiptoe to reach him better. His arms were wrapped tightly around her waist, his lips pressed to the pulse at her neck.

Anjali took a bite of his shoulder and was thrilled to hear him groan in response. She soothed him with the tip of her tongue before looking up at his face, her brown eyes glowing with passion. Water dripped on her forehead from Parth's spiked hair as he gazed at her with his seductive silver eyes. "Sexy cat," he growled before nipping her earlobe.

"Parth, I want you inside me now," she commanded, refusing to wait any longer.

He obliged her every whim before switching off the shower and bundling her in a towelling robe. He towelled the excess water from her hair before drying himself, his eyes clinging to hers.

"I adore you, Parth. Will you marry me?" she whispered; her gaze bold as she studied his glorious nakedness.

She felt his hand in her hair as he pulled her face up to his, "What! You don't plan to go on your knees?"

Anjali laughed, immediately doing just that. She took his right hand in hers and held it against her heart. "Will you make an honest woman of me?" she asked, her eyes devouring him.

He lifted her up in his arms, laughing with glee. "For sure, though I have a condition. Let me have my evil way with you one more time before we tie the knot tomorrow. What do you say?" he wiggled his eyebrows suggestively.

"Yes Parth!"

THE END

OTHER BOOKS
BY
SUNDARI
VENKATRAMAN

SUNDARI
VENKATRAMAN
AMAZON BESTSELLING AUTHOR
MEGHNA

The young and dashing Rahul Sinha lives in England with his parents, Shyam and Rajni. He is an only son of the rich banker. Rahul is totally attached to his father but does not care for his mother. Read the book to find out why….

Rahul is exulted with his efforts at work paying off and plans a holiday with his best friend Sanjay Srivastav who lives in Mumbai with his wife Reema, kids Sasha and Rehaan and most importantly, his sister, Meghna. Rahul recalls meeting Meghna just before they parted six years ago.

Meghna works for a website and also teaches modern dance as she loves it. She's thrown for a toss when Rahul comes visiting. She had thought he had forgotten them.

But how could Rahul do that? Sanjay's his best friend and Rahul had always treated their home as his own. Sanjay's mother had been more of a mother to Rahul than his own. Rahul had stayed away after moving to England or so Meghna believes.

Thus begins the story of Rahul and Meghna, the teasing, the flirting, the anger, the tears…

…will they find love?

SUNDARI
VENKATRAMAN
AMAZON BESTSELLING AUTHOR
Arjun's
PENANCE

*Y*oung Arjun feels betrayed and heartbroken when his girlfriend of two years dies in an accident. In the moment of agony, he does the worst thing possible...

Ten years later, Kiara walks into the office of the Mathur Group of industries, falling for its managing director, Arjun Mathur, who is a ruthless businessman nowadays, and also completely sworn off women.

While the ethical hacker gathers evidence against the ex-finance director of the company who has been swindling money bigtime, she tries to woo the MD into falling in love with her.

Will Kiara be able to persuade Arjun to break his penance?

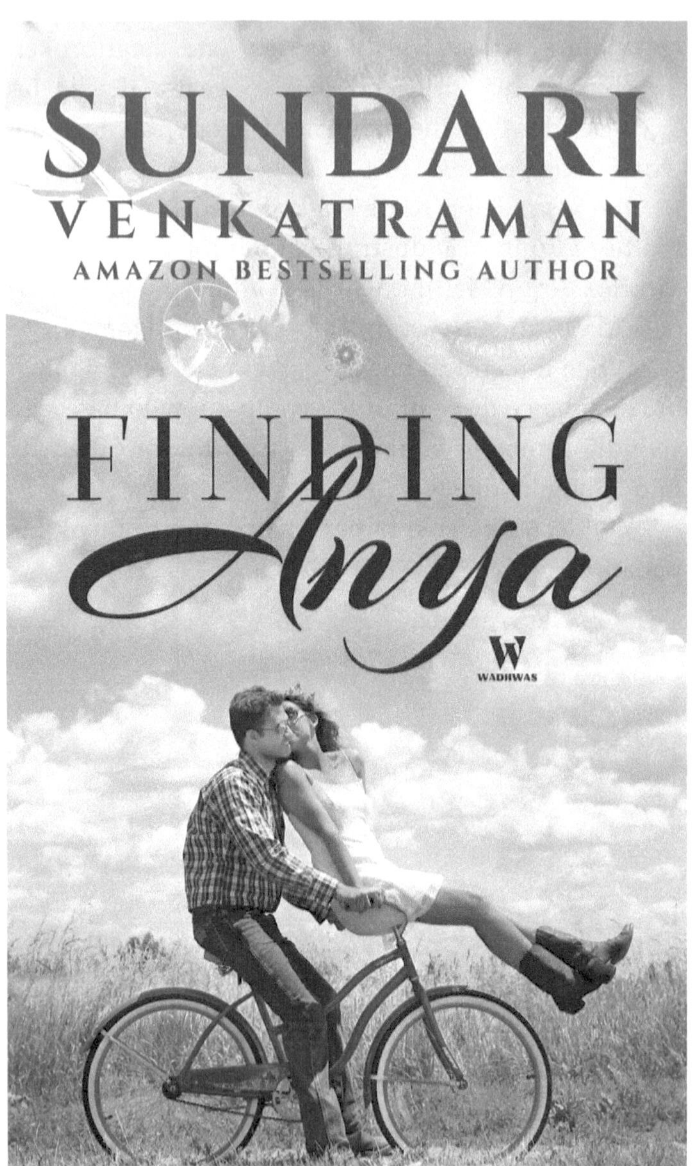
SUNDARI VENKATRAMAN
AMAZON BESTSELLING AUTHOR
FINDING
Anya
W
WADHWAS

nya Chhabria wakes up in a hospital room with no recognition of who she is and where she belongs. In her troubled times, Anya finds her anchor in a handsome stranger. But is he really unknown to her?

Dev Wadhwa's past finds him when he sees Anya lying unconscious in the middle of the road. Not willing to let go of her one more time, Dev takes her to the hospital and later to his farmhouse, where he helps her recuperate.

Sparks fly and Dev and Anya fall for each other! But the feisty Anya refuses to commit herself to marriage as her loss of memory looms larger than life.

Things aren't easy with an ex-husband, not-so-understanding parents, and a jealous neighbour thrown into the mix. What if Anya's memory never comes back?

Will Dev and Anya get a second chance?

Or will circumstances force them apart, yet again?

Connect with Sundari Venkatraman here:

Sundari Venkatraman Books

Sundari Venkatraman Books

https://www.sundarivenkatraman.in

Author Sundari Venkatraman

@sundarivenkat

@sundarivenkatraman

sundarivenkat@gmail.com